Dreamer
Cloning Love

David Nevarez

D&F Books

First Edition, 2025

Published by D&F Books

Cover design and layout by David Nevarez and Firas Bannour

ISBN: 979-8-9988440-1-0

For information, contact:

D&F Books

Riverside, California

U.S. Copyright Registration Case #: 1-14910098631

Special Thanks

Special thanks to my mom, Loida, who inspired me to actually write this book by listening with patience and genuinely enjoying the story. I'll always cherish those moments we spent together. I miss you, Mom.

To my beautiful daughter Mystasia, who kept the story on track whenever I strayed too far—thank you for grounding the heart of this project.

And to my newfound friend Firas Bannour, for guiding some pivotal changes that made this story more suspenseful and exciting.

Chapter 1

Desert Drive

It was Hot! Hot enough to melt dreams into doubts, and Dan had plenty of both. The desert stretched like a fever dream, where heat warped the horizon into watery lies. Cacti stood like frozen thoughts, while a tumbleweed wandered by, dry and aimless. A red sports car suddenly broke the quiet as it sped along the cracked black pavement of I-40, trailing a cloud of dust. Dan reached over to adjust the car's AC, trying to get some relief from the heat outside. Despite the temperature, he couldn't help but smile as the cool air fought back against the desert sun. Veins tightening as he gripped the wheel tighter, eyes fixed on the road. He drove to Arizona, where his new house awaited.

Dan had always wanted to live away from the noise of the city, and this house was everything he'd imagined. The house stood tall and confident against the rocky mountainside, like a desert oasis carved straight from a dream. Its modern lines blended seamlessly into the landscape, with tall windows catching rays of golden sun and flooding the inside with warmth. Leafy desert plants and proud cacti framed the gray stone path that led to the front door, giving the place a rugged, yet peaceful charm. Dan couldn't help but imagine them—he and Christy—lying on a cozy blanket under a sky so full of stars that it seemed painted just for them. The city was far, far away, just a faint glow on the horizon, and here, in this stillness, everything felt possible. He could almost hear the soft rustle of wind brushing past the cacti, feel the cool desert air on his skin, and see Christy's face lit by the bonfire, her smile reflecting every star above. She'd been on his mind the entire trip, and just picturing her here, in this perfect place, made his heart race with anticipation. The house wasn't just a home—it was a promise, a sanctuary, and the beginning of something real.

It had been five years since he last saw her. He was nineteen back then, and she was seventeen. It was 1987, a year of good fortune for him. He had started his dream career in science but had also ended up moving to California, which slowly separated the two of them. Even with all that time and distance, they still kept in touch, mostly through letters or emails. But seeing her again—he couldn't wait. He thought about the moment he first realized how much she meant to him. They were kids, and Christy's older sister Shelly had put a red ant in a black ant's nest, just to watch them fight. While everyone else laughed, Christy was the only one who pleaded with Shelly to stop. The sight of the cruelty was unbearable for her. She bit her lip, her eyes fixed on the tiny red ant struggling below. Finally, Dan reached over, his fingers deftly and gently extracting the struggling red ant and freed it. When he looked up, Christy's face lit up with such genuine gratitude, as she smiled at him with such warmth and sincerity. Dan's heart skipped a beat, a flutter that echoed through his chest. Her expression struck something deep within him. In that moment, an unwavering desire took root within him—a yearning to be her guardian, her protector, a desire which only grew with time. She was beautiful, with long brown hair that reached her mid-back and eyes that were full of innocence and light. But it wasn't just her looks; it was her kindness, the way she admired and respected life. Remembering her made Dan press his foot harder on the accelerator—the speedometer hit 85 mph as the desert flashed past.

When Dan wasn't thinking about Christy, he was thinking about his other love—science. Science filled the spaces in his thoughts, its mysteries capturing him just as much as Christy did. His fascination with electrostatics had started young, and as a teen, he'd spent hours studying its possibilities. It wasn't easy, as most books and literature of the time highlighted the dangers of electrostatic.

Static electricity was a well-documented ignition source as fine dust particles becomes a combustible at that size. Dust explosions in industries such as flour mills, paper mills, grain silos, and wood processing facilities were common as fine dust particles were transported, agitated, or processed, the particles collide and separate repeatedly, leading to charge separation and buildup of static charges within the dust itself—much like how static charge accumulates in a rain cloud causing lightning, igniting the suspended combustible dust, bringing down entire factories.

Dan saw beyond the warnings. He recognized the potential of electrostatics, understanding that while it posed risks, it also offered opportunities for innovation and exploration. His curiosity drove him to delve deeper, seeking applications that could harness electrostatic principles safely and effectively. He'd devised gadgets like battery-powered devices to create miniature lightning, a harmless thrill he often shared with friends. It was Christy who once told him, "That's why I like you. You're a little audacious, but you have a good heart." She whispered. Her words echoed in his mind, and he smirked at the thought. That was Dan: a little audacious, and proud of it. Dan also had one genuine friend, Steven. Steven shared his love for electrostatics, although for him it was more about creating daring, "mad scientist" gadgets. Together, they made many devices: shock gag toys, bug zappers, and flying toys made of aluminum foil. They even sold their inventions at school, earning some pocket money. Steven's dad eventually introduced them to an investor named Frank Pemberton, who saw their potential and helped start a company called "Scientific Incorporated Technologies." He promised to make them partners when they got older. Dan smiled at the memories, feeling a rush of excitement. His life so far had been more than he could have asked for.

He glanced at the road ahead, the air shimmering in waves like the desert itself was breathing. Just 25 miles to Arizona—25 miles to everything he'd been chasing. The horizon danced under the sun's blistering gaze, a rippling mirage that teased him with the promise of a new life. His new high-tech home and a reconciliation with Christy seemed like a far-off dream. Each mile felt like a step deeper into the unknown, a sweltering expanse of heat and hope, daring him to believe that everything he wanted was—just beyond the horizon.

Chapter 2

Moving In and Setting Up

DAN'S MEMORIES FADED AS he finally arrived at his new home. As soon as he pulled up, he saw three enormous trucks parked under the scorching Arizona sun. Men in gray jumpsuit uniforms were loading discarded empty boxes. But behind the thrill of seeing it all come together was a twist of anxiety tightening in his chest. His eyes scanned the scene nervously—had the private crates made its way down to the lab unnoticed? Hidden among ordinary deliveries were pieces of delicate components of his personal project. If anything happened to them—if even one part was lost, damaged, or discovered—his entire plan would collapse before it began. Those containers held everything he'd dreamed of.

Dan's face lit up with excitement as he took in the house's sight, trying to push the worry aside. He parked, turned off the engine, and opened the car door. The heat slammed into him like a furnace, the thick desert air replacing the cool, safe comfort of the AC. Sweat beaded on his forehead immediately, but he didn't care. He was finally here.

Dan walked up the cobbled driveway, imagining how Christy would react when she saw the place. He grinned and greeted a worker as he passed by, who gave a quick nod, beads of sweat rolling off his forehead. Entering the cool shade of his house, Dan let out a sigh of relief. He took a moment to look around the new place, already feeling at home.

"Dan, hey!" a familiar voice called out. Dan looked up to see Bernie, one of Mr. Pemberton's engineers. "This place is awesome! We're all going to miss you at the office, but I have to say, I'm really glad you let me help set up your lab, " Said Bernie, who smiled wide, and Dan couldn't help but smile back. Bernie leaned closer, his voice dropping to a conspiratorial whisper. "I mean, your . Secret Lab...," he added with a wink and a sly grin.

Dan chuckled, nodding. "Thanks, Bernie. I'm glad you could help. I hope it wasn't too much trouble," he said, hands in his pockets as he rocked slightly on his heels.

"Nah, most of it was easy. We got almost everything set up just like you wanted. There are a few more crates that need to go down to the lab, though. You'll need to take them yourself. You know where the elevator is, right?" Bernie asked, handing Dan a clipboard to sign.

He nodded. "Yeah, I've got it."

"Are you sure you don't need help?" Bernie raised an eyebrow.

He shook his head while skimming over the forms. "No, I think I can manage."

Bernie smiled and continued, "We got here early, before anyone else showed up, and we used the stairs for most of the stuff. The elevator was only for the bigger items—when nobody was around, of course. We kept things quiet." Dan looked up and gave him a thankful nod. "You've got a nice setup down there, simple, but very functional. I like it." Bernie Endorsed.

He finished signing the forms and handed the clipboard back. "Yeah, I always wanted something like this when I was a kid. Figured, why not now?" Dan said, his excitement clear despite his casual shrug.

"I'd love one too, but I doubt my wife would let me tear up our house to build a secret lab," Bernie laughed, and Dan joined in with a hearty chuckle.

Bernie suddenly remembered and reached into his pocket. "Oh, almost forgot! These are for you." He handed Dan a small white box. "There are four transducer chips in there. Mr. Pemberton wanted these installed for the keyless entry systems around the house. Just have one of these on you, and if your hands are full, just say 'open' and the doors will unlock and open. There's also a microphone hidden in the doorbell, so it works like an intercom, too. Pretty cool, right?" Bernie pulled out something else—a sleek watch—and handed it over. "There's a small chip there, so you won't need any keys," Bernie continued. Dan smiled as he admired the watch and slipped it around his left wrist. "And one more thing." He grinned, holding out a delicate platinum necklace with a tiny gold heart. "Mr. Pemberton said this is for your 'new girlfriend.'" Bernie said and winked. Dan blushed, taking the necklace. "There's a transducer in the heart, see? Pretty small, huh?" Bernie added, folding his arms and watching Dan's reaction.

Dan cleared his throat, a little embarrassed but clearly touched. "Wow, this is... really nice. I'll have to thank him properly."

"You do that. Anyway, that's it for me. Take care, Dan," Bernie said as he turned to leave, but then paused. "Oh, and by the way, I saw your secretary in there earlier. She did an amazing job, really." Bernie nodded approvingly before heading out.

He waved goodbye; his curiosity piqued. As he made his way inside, he noticed Janet coming down the stairs. "Janet, hey! How's it going?" Dan called out with a smile.

"Hello! Everything is coming along perfectly," Janet said, her face lighting up. She adjusted her glasses and smiled warmly. "Thank you for letting me decorate this place. It's been a dream of mine to work in a house this big. So, what do you think of it so far?" Janet finally asked.

They walked together, and Dan took in the sights. To his right was a spacious family room with a grand fireplace, a big-screen LCD TV, though not available to consumers in the 1980s, and comfortable white furniture. To his left was a cozy sunken living room, perfect for chatting with friends or relaxing with a hot drink. The black couch faced a footrest and end table, with a matching love seat nearby.

"I know you don't drink much, but," Janet gestured toward the bar, where an elegant bottle of whiskey stood. "I thought it'd be a delicate touch, you know, for when you have guests over. Plus, it looks great with the decor!"

He laughed softly. "Yeah, it adds something," he said, setting the bottle back down. They continued exploring, passing the dining room with its elegant oak China cabinet and into the kitchen having polished countertops. Janet watched Dan's reactions closely, clearly proud of her work.

"I love it. It's perfect," Dan finally said, breathing out in satisfaction.

Janet visibly relaxed, a proud smile on her face. "Well, my work is done here," she said proudly.

A loud noise from outside caught Dan's attention. "Hey, where do you want this?" a worker called out, rolling in a large crate. "There's three more in the truck."

"What's in them?" Janet asked, looking puzzled.

The worker shrugged. "Not sure. They're marked 'Very, Very Fragile. CONFIDENTIAL. See Dan.'"

Dan stepped forward, recognizing the crates. "Just put them next to the China cabinet for now. I'll deal with them later," he said.

Janet looked relieved, though a little displeased with placing the bulky crates next to her neatly arranged room. "Suit yourself," the worker said, gesturing for the others to follow him as they wheeled into the crates.

Once everything was in place, Janet signed off on the delivery and turned to Dan. "We're all going to miss you at the office, you know," she said, her voice a little wistful.

"It's just temporary," Dan reassured her, giving her a comforting pat on the shoulder.

Janet pulled him into a quick hug. "Well, if you need anything, just call, okay?" She said and smiled, then followed the workers out, making sure everything was in place before closing the door behind her.

Dan heard the front door lock automatically and took a deep breath. This was home now. Through: Through the small LCD peeping monitor next to the door, he saw them all drive away. A sense of peace washed over him as he smiled. He couldn't wait for Christy to see it. He looked over the crates blocking his way to the China Cabinet. With excitement bubbling inside him, he hurried upstairs to the main bedroom.

The room looked enormous, and Dan couldn't help but explore. He opened the closet door, revealing a full-length mirror. Running his fingers along the top frame, he heard a faint beep from his watch. Suddenly, the mirror slid back, revealing a spiral staircase leading down into darkness.

Dan grinned, glancing back at his room before stepping into the shadows, eager to see what awaited him below.

Chapter 3

Into the Lab

As DAN DUCKED THROUGH the secret doorway, a grin spread across his face. The lights along the railings and steps began lighting up one by one, each additional glow adding to his growing excitement. With every step down the spiral staircase, he felt a jolt of joy. He paused and headed back up to close the mirror door. He tried to slide it shut, but it wouldn't budge. Frowning, he pressed his palm against it and tried again, but with no luck. He sighed, shoulders slumping, until he noticed a small blue button pulsing beside the door. Dan pressed the button, and the door slid closed effortlessly. He chuckled to himself. "Of course there's a button," he muttered, shaking his head before turning back to the steps.

The further down he went, the faster his excitement built. At the base of the stairs was a huge, heavy-looking door. It looked like a door you'd find in a bank vault—solid and imposing. Dan figured someone designed it for fire safety, or maybe even explosion safety, considering the type of work he planned to do here. He pulled down the long handle, and the door swung open with effortless ease.

Dan stepped into the lab, and his eyes widened as the room lit up. Bright white lights revealed a spacious area filled with instruments, some already powered on and glowing softly. He glanced around, noticing the exit sign above the door. "Emergency exit," he murmured. "I guess that explains why there's no lock."

The lab looked spacious, now fully lit. Along the far wall, he could see an open door to a bedroom and a small bathroom. There was also an emergency eyewash fountain and a drench shower in the corner. Along the south wall was a clock over a large acrylic window and a door next to it marked "Safety Room." Dan walked over, placed his hand on the handle. There was a faint beep from his watch, and he heard a click as it unlocked. He grinned as he stepped back, watching the door open. It was cool, but there was nothing new in there that he hadn't already seen through the window, so he moved on.

He walked into the spare bedroom—a place to crash when late nights turned into early mornings, and he didn't feel like going back upstairs. The room was cozy, with a queen-sized bed, a nightstand. There was also a mini fridge stocked with bottled water and fruit juice. A small door led to a private bathroom. Dan nodded in approval. It would do nicely.

On his way out, Dan noticed the elevator to the left of the vaulted door leading up to the stairs. He pressed the button, hearing a faint beep from his watch, and watched the doors slide open, and stepped inside. The elevator rose, the soft light framing the doors fading away as it moved. Dan marveled at the smooth ride, a satisfied smile on his face. When it reached the top, the light shifted to another set of doors. A green "All Clear" sign lit up next to a screen displaying his living room. Dan pressed another blue button, and the doors opened as the China cabinet slid aside silently. He hurried out and pushed in one crate before the doors closed, taking it back down to the lab.

He repeated the process three more times, easily bringing all the crates down. When finished, Dan headed back up to the kitchen. He could have grabbed water from the mini fridge in the lab, but he wanted another excuse to ride the elevator. He felt like a kid who'd just discovered a new toy—the smooth ride, the lights, the secret passage. It all made him feel like the lead in his own sci-fi movie.

Dan wandered into the kitchen, hands in his pockets as he took in the sleek cabinets and shiny floors. He grabbed a glass, walked over to the fridge, and pressed it against the water dispenser. The quiet of the kitchen was almost eerie—all he could hear was the gentle splashing of water and his own breathing. He gulped down the cold water, feeling it cool him from the inside out.

For a moment, he closed his eyes, letting the silence stretch. But in his mind, he filled it—imagining Christy's laughter echoing off the walls, the sound of bare feet padding across the floor, music playing from the living room while something sweet baked in the oven. He pictured her spinning in the kitchen with a playful smile, the scent of cinnamon or something buttery filling the air. This place was quiet now, but in his heart, it was already alive—with warmth, with joy, with her. The thought pulled at him, soft and aching. It was the togetherness he longed for most.

Setting the glass down, Dan glanced at the grandfather clock just as it struck 1:30. Right on cue, his stomach growled. He was definitely hungry.

Chapter 4

Duplicating a Dream

DAN DROVE TEN MILES to the nearest supermarket. The only upside was that the car ride gave him time to think. His mind kept circling back to Christy. He sighed, her name on his lips.

Christy had been Dan's childhood friend; someone he had always cherished. But lately, he'd struggle with risking their friendship by pursuing a romantic relationship. Her recent letters hinted at her interest in Mark—a guy Dan couldn't stand. Mark was arrogant, manipulative, and had a reputation for playing with girls' emotions. Dan clenched his jaw just thinking about it. He couldn't understand how Christy, someone so smart and kind, could be interested in someone like Mark.

Dan relaxed his grip on the steering wheel, releasing a heavy sigh. Christy had said that Mark seemed different now, that he was trying to be a better person, even working as a vacuum cleaner salesperson. But Dan knew better. Mark had always been a charmer, convincing girls to trust him and take advantage of them before inevitably breaking their hearts. He had a feeling Mark hadn't changed at all.

As he drove, Dan spotted the road leading to Christy's house. He thought of stopping by, imagining the bright smile that always greeted him. It took all his willpower to keep driving, knowing it wasn't time yet. He didn't want to mess up his plan.

Dan's plan was simple in his mind, though others might think it was a bit out there. He recalled his conversation with his best friend Steven just before he moved.

"Christy?! Again? When is this crush gonna end?" Steven had said, exasperated. "She doesn't even know you like her. And besides, didn't you tell me she's into some other guy?"

"Yeah," Dan replied, hiding his frustration. "Some so-called cool guy.'"

"What's wrong with that? I mean, I'm kind of a cool guy," Steven teased, a smirk on his face.

Dan rolled his eyes. "You at least let girls know what they're getting into. Mark lies to them, and when he's done, he just leaves them."

Steven nodded, agreeing. "Yeah, he's a creep. But listen, she's out of state. Long-distance relationships never work." Steven paused, his eyes narrowing. "Wait... Arizona.. Is that why you're moving there?"

Dan smiled, embarrassed. "Yeah, it is."

"Dan, come on! You're giving everything up for a girl," Steven said, shaking his head.

"I know it sounds crazy, but I have a plan. A sure thing! It has to work," Dan insisted, though even he was trying to convince himself.

Steven crossed his arms. "How can you be so sure? Relationships are unpredictable."

Dan paused, thinking about Steven's words. "I've thought this through a hundred times, Steven. I have a project at home that could make this work without risking her friendship. It's almost foolproof." He smiled, his excitement shining through.

"What project?" Steven asked, curiosity piqued.

"I've been working on a way to duplicate matter," Dan said, his voice dropping to a whisper.

Steven looked at him in disbelief. "A matter duplicator? Are you serious? And you almost have it working?"

Dan nodded. "Well, not exactly, but I'm close. Once it's ready, I'll use it to make a copy of Christy. That way, I can learn more about her without risking anything. It's like a trial run. Then, if things go well, I can un- copy her, then talk to her for real." Dan's excitement was obvious, though he could see Steven was unconvinced.

"Dan, this is too much! You're building a revolutionary machine! — a matter duplicator! — and you're using it to dupe a girl? You could change the world with this thing!" Steven argued.

"I know. But she's worth it," Dan mumbled. "I don't want to make any mistakes! I need this to work!"

Steven sighed. "Okay, man. If anyone can pull it off, it's you. But it still sounds crazy. Why not just talk to her like a normal person?"

Dan shook his head. "I've tried. Every time, I mess it up. I get nervous and awkward, and she ends up thinking we're just friends. This way, I can figure it out without risking what we already have."

Steven looked at Dan, seeing the determination in his friend's eyes. He placed a hand on Dan's shoulder. "Alright. I hope it works out for you. Just... don't lose yourself in all this." Dan smiled in appreciation.

Dan pulled into the supermarket parking lot, his conversation with Steven still echoing in his mind. The heat hit him like a wall as he stepped out of his car. He quickly locked the car and made his way toward the store, pausing under a canopy with a misting fan. He let the cool mist wash over him, smiling at a young couple selling personalized mugs and t-shirts nearby. After a quick nod to them, he walked inside, grateful for the blast of AC.

He grabbed a shopping cart and headed to the fruit section, his thoughts still on Christy and his plan. He filled bags with apples, oranges, tomatoes, and a head of lettuce when a voice startled him.

"Dan!?" He turned, not recognizing the voice at first. "It's me, Tina. Christy's friend," Tina said, giving him a smile.

Dan remembered Tina well. She was always a bit... intense. With an almost supernatural ability, she could read people as if she could see right through them. She was blunt but kind and honest, and Dan could see why Christy liked her so much. "Hi, Tina," Dan said, trying to hide his nervousness. He knew she could tell he wasn't entirely comfortable. She always seemed to know. "Is Christy here?" he asked, hoping she wasn't.

"No, she's out with Mark," Tina said, rolling her eyes. "I can't stand that guy, so I decided to get some errands done. I hate leaving them alone for too long, though." She sighed. Dan clenched his jaw at the mention of Mark, but he appreciated Tina seemed to be on his side. "You're looking a little thin," she said, looking him over. "Does Christy know you're in town?"

"No, not yet," Dan replied, stuttering slightly. "I wanted to surprise her. I had a house built in our favorite spot up the mountains." He fumbled in his pocket for a card and handed it to Tina. "Here's my number."

Tina took the card, studying it for a moment. "You should call her soon. She'd be happy to see you," she said, giving him a quick smile before heading off. "Anyway, I've got to go. I need to catch up with Christy before Mark gets too comfortable." She patted his shoulder and walked away, leaving Dan feeling a little more hopeful.

Dan continued shopping, grabbing some frozen dinners, eggs, and bread. After paying, he walked out, feeling the rush of hot air as the doors opened. He hurried to his car, packed up the groceries, and started the engine, letting the AC blast away the heat.

As he drove home, Dan thought again about his conversation with Steven. He remembered Steven's disbelief when Dan mentioned duplicating Christy. "Why not just win her over with what you already know about her?" Steven had asked. But Dan wanted more than that—he wanted to be sure to avoid mistakes. The duplicator wasn't just about love—it was about certainty. And even though Dan had countless reservations about the ethics, the risk, the sheer insanity of it all, there was no surer way to get it right. No margin for error. No second chances. Only this.

Dan parked in his driveway and carried in the groceries. He missed Steven, but his thoughts quickly shifted back to Christy. He had hope—a plan. Finishing the duplicator was all that remained. Then, maybe, he could finally be with the girl he'd always loved.

Chapter 5

Assembling The Duplicator

THE DUPLICATING UNIT WAS a marvel of technology, each component meticulously crafted to bring Dan's vision to life. His enthusiasm was evident as he eagerly pried open the first crate labeled "A". Inside was a sophisticated Analog Crystal Supercomputer, naturally developed by Dan's company, Scientific Incorporated Technologies. The circuits were engineered for fast and accurate data processing, making it ideal for his project's requirements.

Unlike standard computers, this analog powerhouse processed complex calculations using frequencies and signals, interfacing seamlessly with the electro-optic scanners and bioelectric sensors Dan needed.

All the programs Dan had designed were critical, but the most important was the Monitoring Program. It had one job: to monitor the massive amount of data being gathered. This wasn't just simple information—it included the makeup of every single microscopic element of Christy's body. It mapped out all ten trillion cells, including their DNA, the bio-electromagnetic fields they produced, and much more. The Monitoring Program meticulously ensured that every detail remained intact, for even the slightest error could set off a chain reaction that could alter everything.

Unpacking the remaining crates revealed Crystal Data Drives, provided by Scientific Incorporated Technologies as well. These drives, best described as a holographic data storage units, were crucial because of their ability to store several exabytes of data in a small, compact form.

Also inside the crate was an external scanning platform, with each component contributing to the complex assembly. Dan found himself particularly fascinated by the platform's golden, birdcage-like structure. Hexagonal sensors, capable of detecting bioelectric signatures from individual cells, equipped the platform; this was crucial for recreating the fine details of a living being.

Dan imagined Christy standing on the platform, her graceful figure framed perfectly within the golden structure. The vision was so vivid, so real, that it sent a shiver through him, resonating with both anticipation and awe. He could almost see the sensors spark to life as they captured every intricate detail of her being, from the luminous flow of her hair to the gentle rhythm of her heartbeat. The thought of recreating something so precious, so uniquely her, filled him with a heady mix of excitement and wonder. It was as if the entire machine existed solely for that moment when it would hold Christy in its delicate grasp, and the enormity of it left him breathless. This was not just a technological marvel; it extended his deepest desires, a testament to how far he will go to bridge the chasm between his logical world and the emotional connection he yearned for. The anticipation was almost unbearable, but it also fueled him, driving him to complete his work.

As the last pieces clicked into place, Dan stood back, admiring his creation—a machine that symbolized both his ambition and his love for Christy. Exhausted but exhilarated, he stifled a yawn, feeling the weight of his long hours. "Time to call it a day," he murmured, sliding the data drives into their slots before heading to bed.

When morning came, sunlight pouring through the windows, Dan wasted no time getting back to his lab. He wanted to make sure everything was still in place from the night before. He went through each connection, visually confirming that everything looked good. Then, he set up a diagnostics program to check every intricate connection and make sure all the hardware and data drives were functioning properly. This would catch any issues he might have missed.

The diagnostics program was running smoothly... Dan's stomach rumbled, reminding him he hadn't eaten. He decided it was time for a quick break. Having checked the screen to make sure everything was still running, he then briefly rode the elevator to the kitchen. He grabbed an apple, savoring the juicy crunch as he bit into it, and took a second apple for later. Then he headed back down to the basement, eager to keep working.

Hours went by as Dan meticulously examined every line of code the program generated. He focused intently. When the diagnostics finally finished, showing no errors, Dan scanned through the report to confirm. Satisfied, he connected the platform to the supercomputer.

Dan rubbed the back of his neck, stretching as he ran another set of validation programs. They all passed with no issues, but he realized it was now past lunchtime. With a sigh, he took the elevator up to grab a quick TV dinner, leaving it to cool on the counter while he went back down to the lab.

He grew restless as he continued running diagnostics for each crucial step—scanning, recording, duplicating. It was time-consuming, but Dan knew it was necessary. By the time he finished, evening had arrived, and his forgotten lunch sat cold on the counter—a small price for the accomplishment he'd achieved.

Back in the lab, he completed the data, and a smile spread across his face. The green glow on the screen confirmed everything had run smoothly. Everything was finally ready. Now, it was time for the fun part!

Chapter 6

Experiments and Failures

AFTER SPENDING MORE TIME troubleshooting, Dan retrieved his notes and realized that the real challenge wasn't in de-materializing or re-materializing an object. Each atom had its own "memory," a natural bond that made it want to stay in place. No, the real problem was in maintaining the stability of those processes during duplication, without interfering with the electrical charges or bonds between atoms.

Dan decided it was time to test the next step. He pressed the Scan button, and the machine hummed to life. The platform made a single, smooth rotation before coming to a stop. Dan caught a faint whiff of ozone, a sharp and metallic scent that showed an electrical charge in the air. He checked the logs, made a few calibrations, and tried again. Once more, the platform rotated with deliberate precision, and this time, he observed a successful reading of "nothing." However, this was not "nothing" in the sense of complete absence, but the "nothing" that encompassed the subtle presence of air, swirling dust particles, and the invisible elements that inhabit what we might consider empty space. This meant the system was working properly.

"Yes!" Dan shouted, his voice echoing in the quiet lab. It was a minor success, but it was progress. He made a few notes about how this technology could revolutionize medical scanning, allowing doctors to detect tiny, almost invisible particles in the body. Feeling energized, Dan was ready to take the next step.

He looked around the lab for something to scan and noticed the bright red apple sitting on his desk he had brought down the other day. He picked it up and placed it on the platform. With a deep breath, Dan pressed the Scan button. The machine came alive, and the platform made full rotation. Much more detailed data came through this time. The log recorded every part of the apple, down to the tiniest molecule. Dan saved the data and marveled at the intricate patterns, almost as if the apple had its own story to tell.

HE TOOK THE APPLE off the platform and put it back on the desk. Now came the real challenge—creating a duplicate. Behind the acrylic window of the safety room, he stood before a computer that mirrored the one in the lab. He pressed the Duplicate button. He held his breath as the platform spun, a small, blurry shape beginning to form. Dan's heart pounded as he watched, barely able to blink. The shape continued to form, but then it collapsed into a pile of sludge. Dan let out a deep breath, both disappointed and amazed. He hurried a scan of the air around the sludge to ensure there were no toxic substances.

"No dangerous gases, that's good," Dan muttered. He left the safety room to collect a sample of the sludge. It wasn't what he had hoped for, but it was still something. He took the sample to the chemical lab for testing, confirming that it was non-toxic. Though it wasn't an apple, Dan was still excited—he had created something out of nothing.

He cleaned the platform, sat down with the logs, and tried to figure out what went wrong. He tried duplicating the apple a few more times, tweaking the settings with each attempt, but the results were always the same—just more sludge. Frustrated, Dan flopped down on the bed in the lab's small bedroom, holding the log above his face. He read through the notes until his eyelids grew heavy, and sleep took over.

The next day brought fresh energy. Dan freshened up in the room's restroom before he resumed the trials, running scan after scan, scrutinizing every error in hopes of a breakthrough. Hunger eventually forced him to take a break, but his refrigerator was empty, a reminder of his neglected routines. Grabbing a quick refreshing shower, he drove to the market, trying to clear his mind.

The trip seemed shorter than usual, and he found himself absent-mindedly wandering the aisles, grabbing essentials—milk, bread, eggs, fruit. He caught a glimpse of his reflection and chuckled, thinking he looked like a frustrated zombie, pushing his cart around in no general direction.

As he was finishing up his shopping, he overheard a girl at the register giggling. "Mark, stop it! I'm working," she said. Dan's smile vanished, and his head shot up. There was Mark, standing at the counter with a confident smirk. He looked different from how Dan remembered him—taller, more built, with a casual swagger. Dan's heart sank as he watched Mark wink at the cashier before turning to leave.

Dan's stomach twisted with anxiety. Was this the same Mark that Christy was seeing? He tried to push the thought away, but it lingered, making him feel nauseous. He grabbed a TV dinner and a pot pie, paid for his groceries, and hurried out of the store. As he loaded the bags into his car, he noticed Mark lingering, flirting with another girl while getting into his black Firebird, then speeding off. While looking in Mark's direction, Dan noticed a pet shop nearby. A strange idea popped into his head—maybe he needed to branch out in his experiments. A live subject, like a mouse or a rat, might be the key.

Inside the pet shop, Dan learned they didn't carry mice anymore, but they had a small white rabbit. After some bargaining, Dan bought the rabbit, along with a cage, water dispenser, and food—all at a discount. He drove home with the rabbit in the back seat, his mind already racing with new possibilities.

Back at home, Dan hurried the groceries into the fridge and set up the rabbit's cage in the lab. "Welcome to your new home," he said, squeezing a few leaves of lettuce through the cage bars. The rabbit nibbled at the lettuce, its nose twitching, and Dan smiled. He felt a renewed sense of energy—maybe this rabbit would be the breakthrough he needed.

He returned to the platform, but none of his new ideas worked. Each attempt ended in the same way—just more sludge. Frustrated, Dan placed the log aside. "It's not even applesauce!" He said out loud. He looked at the rabbit, peacefully dozing in its cage, and sighed. He took a break and headed upstairs.

In the kitchen, Dan noticed the answering machine blinking. He pressed play, and Tina's voice filled the room. "Hey Dan, it's Tina. When are you going to call Christy? I told her you were in town. Call her, bone-head." Dan deleted the message without hesitation. He didn't need Tina pressuring him right now.

Frustrated by the lack of progress, Dan put a TV dinner and a pot pie in the oven, opting to go outside while they baked. The sky, now a deep gray, almost black in some places, loomed on the horizon, casting a gloomy shadow over everything below. Lightning flickered in the distance, illuminating the dark sky for a split second. The distant rumble of thunder echoes through the sky, a low growl that gradually grows louder. A small breeze picks up, heavy with the scent of rain, a fresh, earthy smell that mingled with the sharp tang of ozone from the impending storm. The smell of wet weeds and wild plants mixed in, creating a nostalgic aroma. It reminded him of the times he spent with Christy next to the Colorado River, just the two of them exploring and having fun. His heart ached at the memory, and his thoughts shifted back to Mark. Was he losing Christy to that guy?

The dinner was ready when Dan returned inside. He ate rapidly, puffing on each mouthful to cool it down. His mind was already back on the duplicator. He went to the basement, determined to figure out what was missing. He grabbed an orange and placed it on the platform. The scan completed, but once again, it only produced more sludge. This time, though, Dan noticed a small breeze coming from the platform. The surrounding air seemed to be pushed out by the sludge as it formed, which seemed like a clue, though he wasn't sure what it meant. He tried again with different type fruits—a tomato, a banana—but the results were the same. Each time, the duplicator flickered and failed, reducing the samples to unrecognizable mush. The lights above buzzed weakly as the storm outside roared louder, thunder shaking the windows. "What am I doing wrong?" Dan muttered, his voice tight. He kicked at the air, pacing in circles before stopping to yank at his hair in frustration. His brain raced, trying to untangle the science—maybe the static fields were interacting with natural fields in the samples? But from where?! Or was that just another guess in a pile of dead ends?

What made it worse was seeing Mark earlier that day—flirting with the cashier at the store, charming her effortlessly. Dan didn't know for sure if it was the Mark Christy had mentioned... but deep down, he was almost certain. And if it was, then time was running out. Dan felt the pressure mounting, the desperation clinging to him like the humidity in the lab. Every failed test, every sputter of the machine, felt like watching his chances slip through his fingers. The duplicator had to work. It had to! He couldn't let Mark win—not again. Not with Christy. He was finding it difficult to focus.

After hours of failure, Dan finally gave up for the night. The machine stood in silence, cold and useless. He rode the elevator upstairs, defeated and lost. He slumped down at the bar. Rain hammered the windows, lightning slicing through the sky. It was almost 3 a.m., and he felt completely disappointed—exhausted, aggravated, and heartbreakingly alone. Mark's smug face flashed in his mind again, and for a moment, Dan felt insignificant. He stared at the bottle of whiskey for a long moment, then quietly poured himself a shot, the glass trembling slightly in his hand.

Not being much of a drinker and not familiar with whiskey, he swallowed it all in one gulp. The liquid burned down his throat. The grandfather clock struck three. BOOM!... A bright flash of lightning lit up the room immediately followed by a loud crash of thunder making the house shake. Shocked by everything happening all at once, Dan stumbled backward, his foot catching on the barstool, falling to the ground. Pain shot through head then his side, knocking the wind out of him. He tried to get up, but his head spun, and he collapsed back down. Before he could regain his senses, darkness swallowed him whole.

Chapter 7

The Breakthrough

Dan blinked against the sunlight filtering through the drapes, his body stiff from a night spent on the floor. Slowly, he sat up, feeling a dull ache throb through his head as he remembered the previous night's chaos. He winced, reaching back to find a tender bump on his head. With a groan, he hauled himself up, steadying himself with the couch.

Noticing the grandfather clock showing it was already one in the afternoon; Dan shook off the grogginess. After a few slow steps to the bar to collect himself, he braved the climb upstairs to the bathroom. With each step, the fear of losing Christy and the realization of a life without her seemed to intensify the pain. The refreshing shower helped ease the pain and clear his thoughts, and as he splashed water on his face, a sudden realization struck him.

"That's it!" Dan shouted, his face breaking into a smile. He hurried to his closet, quickly put on some clothes, and took the secret staircase to the lab. He moved too quickly, and pain pulsed through his head, forcing him to stop and steady himself. Taking a deep breath, Dan continued down, this time more carefully.

"How did I not realize this before?" Dan muttered as he entered the lab and approached the duplicator. "The electrostatic field from the scanning sensors must be creating interference. It's distorting the target space and messing up the entire process." He shook his head, almost laughing at how simple it seemed now.

He turned toward the small white rabbit sitting in the lab's corner, chewing lazily on a piece of lettuce. "Okay, listen up," Dan said, pointing dramatically at the duplicator. "You know how this thing scans stuff before copying it? Well, turns out, the energy field it gives off is, like, totally messing everything up." The rabbit twitched its nose.

"I'm serious!" Dan grinned. "It's warping the space around whatever I'm trying to duplicate—kind of like how heat makes the road look all wavy in the summer. The scanner's trying to place a clear picture, but the distortion makes it all fuzzy and wrong, so the copy ends up... well, icky and gross."

He paced a little, gesturing with excitement. "So now, I just need to rework the scanner so it doesn't fry the space before it duplicates stuff. Easy, right?" He shot the rabbit a hopeful look. "This could actually work!" he muffled to himself

Dan opened up the duplicator's control panel. "If I turn off the monitoring program during replication, that should stop the interference. Then I can re-enable it to check the result." He set to work, reconfiguring the system, his excitement growing. Once everything was ready, he restored the power, grabbed the apple, and placed it on the scanning plate.

Taking a deep breath before pressing the scan button. The machine hummed to life; the platform rotating smoothly as the scan completed. He set the apple on the desk and pressed the duplicate button, his eyes fixed on the machine, completely missing the warning message flashing on the screen. Nothing happened. Dan frowned, pressing the button again. Still nothing. Confused, he turned to the terminal and saw the error log.

"Oh, right... the scan failed because I disabled the monitoring program," Dan muttered under his breath, scratching his chin with growing anxiety. Suddenly, a flash of inspiration hit him like a bolt of lightning. "Wait... I can use the scan log I saved a few days ago!" he exclaimed, his voice tinged with urgency. With determined precision, he retrieved the stored data, made swift yet meticulous modifications, and inserted it into the replication program. Heart pounding, Dan held his breath and pressed the duplicate button, his fingers crossed in desperate hope.

The platform turned, and Dan watched as a shadowy shape formed. He held his breath, his eyes wide, not daring to blink. The shape slowly solidified, and a bright light flashed over the surface. Dan's heart pounded as he stepped closer. There, on the platform, was an apple—not sludge, but a real solid apple.

Dan's eyes widened, quickly glancing at the apple on his desk, filled with awe and disbelief as he stared at the apple resting solidly on the platform. His hand moved instinctively, fingers trembling slightly, heart hammering with anticipation as he grasped the fruit—solid, cool, and undeniably real. Its skin was smooth under his touch, a tangible proof of his success. With precision and purpose, Dan carefully sliced into the apple, the sweet fresh scent filling the lab, mingling with a quiet rustle. A grin broke across Dan's face—a rush of excitement as his disbelief gave way to exhilaration, reinforcing the realization that his wildest dreams were finally within reach.

With excitement bubbling inside him, Dan sliced off a small piece of the apple and hesitated for a moment before taking a bite. He glanced at the rabbit, its nose twitching with curiosity. "Let's see if this fairy tale has a happy ending," he murmured, extending the slice towards the rabbit. The rabbit nibbled at the apple, its whiskers twitching in delight. Dan watched intently, checking the clock as seconds ticked by. Every detail seemed normal: the rabbit showed no signs of distress, only eagerness for more.

Satisfied, Dan grabbed the other piece of the apple. "The final test," he whispered to himself. He took a deep breath and bit into the apple. Dan's mouth watered as the sweet aroma of the apple intensified, filling his senses with delicious anticipation. The firm flesh yielded gently beneath his teeth, the soft crunch echoing through the lab and sending a thrill of excitement through him. A grin spread across his face, laughter bubbling up as each bite erased lingering doubts, leaving only the pure, sweet taste of success. He savored the moment, exhilarated by the reality of his achievement and the joy that surged within him. "Alright!

Dan!" he yelled out loud, laughing. "It worked! Yes! It worked!" With a chuckle, he handed the rest of the apple to the rabbit, who eagerly accepted the treat.

He documented his findings, his hands shivering with excitement. Dan spent the rest of the night reprogramming the duplicator. He set it so the monitoring program would shut off during replication, then turn back on afterward to ensure everything was flawless. Exhausted but relieved, he looked at the clock and saw it was three in the morning.

Yawning, Dan placed the unit's batteries on the charger, wanting everything ready by morning. He walked to the spare bedroom in the lab. Despite the room's intended purpose for nights like this, he cleaned it rather than sleeping. He made the bed, fluffed the pillows, and ensured the mini-fridge was stocked. Finally satisfied, Dan washed up and turned off the lights, heading upstairs for some well-deserved rest.

Chapter 8

On the Edge of Discovery and Desire

Dan squinted as warm sunlight poured across his face, waking him from sleep. He instinctively touched the back of his head, gingerly feeling the swelling from his fall the previous night. As he sat up carefully, a wave of excitement coursed through him. Throwing the covers aside, and a quick freshen up, he hurried to the closet, making his way to the hidden staircase leading down to the lab.

He hesitated, torn between the urge to share his groundbreaking discovery with Steven and the unsettling realization of its potential misuse. The duplicator, if it fell into the wrong hands, could unleash havoc—counterfeit currency, cloned weapons. The anxiety of its dangerous possibilities overshadowed the excitement of his achievement. With this realization, he needed to proceed with caution. His thoughts shifted to Christy. He had to make sure the machine was safe before attempting anything with her. The thought of a failed duplication ending in disaster was unbearable.

In the lab, Dan approached the rabbit cage, opening it gently. He picked up the small, warm rabbit. With a pang of guilt, he set it on the scanning platform. But the rabbit immediately hopped off, making him chuckle. "Feisty, aren't you?" he murmured, retrieving some lettuce to coax it into place. As the rabbit nibbled contentedly, Dan executed the scan, and the log quickly populated with extensive detailed information.

When the scan completed, he removed the rabbit, placed it back in its cage, and took a deep breath. He pressed the duplicate button. The platform spun, a shape formed, and, to his amazement, a rabbit appeared—complete with a piece of lettuce dangling from its mouth. Marking the duplicate with a black dot, he placed it in the cage with the original. "You've got a new friend," Dan said to the rabbits as he watched, tense, as the original rabbit darted toward the duplicate. Dan half-expected them to attack each other. But the rabbit stopped and peacefully shared the lettuce dangling from its double's mouth. Dan sighed in relief, shaking his head as he watched the two rabbits nibble on their shared meal. "Here's some more," he said, adding more lettuce to the cage. "Enjoy, little guys. I've got work to do."

Dan packed the duplicator into a portable case, grabbed a breakfast bar, and headed out to his car, excitement and nerves mounting as he drove to Christy's house.

The drive to Christy's seemed shorter than he expected, his heart pounding harder the closer he got. As he parked outside her house, Dan swallowed, his fingers lingering on the keys in the ignition. He took a deep breath, trying to build up the courage to get out of the car. But before he could, the screen door swung open, and there she was. Christy. Dan's heart skipped a beat as he watched her step out, her eyes scanning the car until they landed on him. Her face lit up, her mouth breaking into a delighted smile. "Danny?" she called, her voice bright and filled with surprise. Dan's face turned red as he clumsily searched for the car door handle. He tried to open the door, but the door remained locked. He let out a nervous laugh, unlocked it, and got out, only to be pulled back awkwardly by his seatbelt. Christy approached with a giggle and a sparkle in her eyes, asking, "What are you doing here?"

"Christy, Hi! Uh, I, uh, wanted to... surprise you!" Dan stammered, finally getting out of the car. He reached out to shake her hand, but she ignored it, pulling him into a hug instead. He stiffened for a moment, then relaxed, wrapping his arms around her. Her warmth, her scent—everything about her made his mind go blank. He wanted to tell her how much he had missed her, how happy he was to see her, but the words got stuck in his throat. Instead, he just smiled, feeling foolish.

"It's been so long," Christy said, stepping back but still holding his hands. "How are you?"

Dan opened his mouth, the words swirling in his head. He wanted to tell her everything—about the house, the lab, the duplicator—but all he managed was, "I'm fine," followed by a nervous smile.

Christy nodded, her eyes studying him. "You look great," she said warmly. "Do you want something to drink? Water, maybe?"

Dan nodded, grateful for the offer. "Sure, water sounds good." Christy led him inside, calling out, "Mom! You'll never guess who's here!" Dan followed her in, feeling a rush of nostalgia. The house looked the same as it always had, and he smiled at the sight of Christy's little sister, Kathy, playing on the floor. She looked up at Dan shyly before turning her attention back to her toys. "Hey you," Dan said, kneeling down to Kathy, "Christy told me about you, glad to meet you, I'm Dan," he introduced himself, gently tapping her little nose.

Christy's mom, Linda, stepped out from the kitchen, her eyes widening when she saw Dan. "Oh my goodness, Danny! Look at you!" she said, drying her hands on a dish towel. "It's been so long! How are you?"

Dan stood up and chuckled. "I'm doing well, Linda. It's really good to see you again."

She gave him a polite smile, her eyes briefly scanning the layout of the house. "You've been hiding out here, huh? It suits you."

He nodded, then glanced over at Christy, who stepped forward with a glass of cold water. "Here," she said warmly.

"Thanks," he replied, accepting the glass. The sight of her made his heart swell. There was a comfort in her presence that pulled at him. He looked away quickly, trying not to let it show.

He took a sip, then cleared his throat. He knew it was time. "So, um, I've been working on something," he began, trying to sound casual even. "It's a kind of 3D imaging device. It scans and creates digital models—like for mugs, shirts, maybe even display pieces."

He immediately winced internally. That sounded way too vague.

"Oh, like those kiosks at the mall that let you make a bobblehead out of yourself?" Christy asked, perking up with interest.

"Sort of," Dan said, grateful for the save. He forced a laugh and rolled with it. "But this is a bit more... evolved. Instead of just a static figure, it captures the person—full-body—and renders it into a holographic 3D image."

Christy blinked. "Wait, so like... a digital version of me I could see floating in the air?"

"Exactly," Dan nodded, easing into the pitch. "And it's not just frozen in one pose, either. One scan is all it takes, and you can then pose the digital model however you like. Turn the head, move the arms, even make it walk or wave."

Linda raised an eyebrow. "That sounds expensive."

"It's still early," Dan replied, glancing between them. "Right now, I've just been testing it on objects—basic stuff. I had this old mug from college. Scanned it in, and on the screen, I could rotate it, zoom in, change the lighting—it looked more real than the real one."

Christy smiled. "That's kind of amazing. Could you scan people the same way?"

Dan hesitated for half a second too long. "Theoretically, yes. Calibration allows it to recognize textures, depth, and body contours. Similar to a camera, but it doesn't just take a picture though. It layers the subject, building it up. It's all about engagement," Dan said smoothly, falling into the sales pitch he hadn't realized he'd rehearsed. "Imagine a jewelry store display. First you see a hunk of coal—black, rough. Then, it shimmers and rotates, transforming mid-air into a perfect diamond."

Christy's eyes widened. "That's actually... really cool."

"Right?" he said, trying to suppress the guilt rising in his chest. "It gets people's attention. That's the goal."

She leaned against the edge of the kitchen counter, still holding her drink. "So, what else can it do?"

Dan shook his head. "Right now, just the basics. It's all about refining the scan. Lighting, stability, making sure it doesn't glitch out if the subject moves during capture."

Linda narrowed her eyes slightly. "So, it's capturing the image of someone with rotating cameras?"

Dan's grip on the glass tightened slightly. "Exactly. It's all visual. Just a hologram. No sound, no behavior—nothing like that." He gave a small laugh.

"Wow, that sounds amazing! Can I see it?" Christy asked, her enthusiasm making Dan's heart race.

"Ch-Sure! I brought it with me. " Trying to keep from stuttering "If-f you want, you could be my model. It'll only take a few minutes to set up." He pointed outside, already heading towards the door. Christy followed eagerly, and her mom, holding Kathy, watched from the porch, curious.

DAN QUICKLY SET UP the scanner on the rocky lawn. Christy watched, her curiosity growing. "What's this part?" she asked, pointing to the platform.

"That's the scanning plate," Dan explained. "You stand on it while it turns, and the sensors do the rest." He avoided giving too much detail, worried that she might catch on to what the machine was truly capable of.

Christy nodded, stepping onto the platform. Dan helped her up, his hands brushing against hers. She smiled at him. "I like it when you talk about technical stuff. You sound so confident—like in your letters," she said, her eyes twinkling.

Dan blushed, trying to keep his focus. "Okay, just stand still and try to keep balanced," he said. "You might feel a little dizzy or disoriented, like if you're someplace else. But it's perfectly safe." Christy gave him a playful eye roll, but she nodded. Dan looked at his watch, triggering Christy to look at hers. It was a little after 11:52am.

Dan pressed the button, and the scanner hummed to life. The plate turned smoothly, and Christy stood perfectly still. When the scan finished, she stepped off, smiling. "That wasn't bad at all! What was all that about dizziness or being disoriented?"

Dan laughed, scratching his head. "I was just trying to make it sound more exciting," he admitted. Christy giggled, shaking her head. The screen door slammed shut as Linda stepped back in from the porch.

Dan started packing up the machine, but as he did, he noticed a black Firebird pulling up. His heart sank. He knew who it was before he even saw the driver—Mark.. "Oh, I didn't know he was coming over," Christy said quietly, her smile faltering slightly.

He watched as Mark got out, his confident swagger making Dan's heart sink. Christy turned, her face lighting up as she saw him. "Oh, hey." Christy greeted.

"Hey, Chris," Mark said casually, barely sparing a glance in Dan's direction. Christy smiled nervously and gestured between them. "Mark, this is Dan—remember I told you?"

Mark turned to Dan with a smirk and a raised brow. "So, you're the pen pal?" he said, smirking, emphasizing the word like it was some kind of inside joke. Dan forced a polite nod, though his gut twisted at the condescending tone.

Mark's eyes landed on the duplicator. He tilted his head, scoffing. "What's up with the birdcage?" he asked, pointing at the machine like it was some kind of junkyard art piece. His smirk deepened, proud of what he thought was a clever dig.

Dan glanced at him, biting back a sarcastic reply. He just smiled—tight and wordless—and turned his attention to disassembling the machine, pretending the jab had gone over his head. Christy, sensing the awkward tension, tried to step in. "It's actually part of a project Dan's working on. It's really impressive—"

But Mark waved it off with a chuckle. "Right, right? I'm sure..." He rolled his eyes, then looked back at Christy. "Anyways, d'you have ten bucks? Me and the guys are going out for drinks, and I don't want to be short."

Dan watched as Christy hesitated. Mark already had his arm around her shoulders, steering her toward the house like Dan wasn't even there. Dan said nothing, just stood there wishing he had come up with something clever to have said.

Christy turned to Dan. "Please don't go yet. I want to chat some more," she said and then went inside. Dan gritted his teeth, feeling annoyed. He observed Mark, who stood tall and self-assured, which made him feel insignificant. However, when Christy flashed him a hopeful smile, he found himself unable to leave.

Christy returned with Mark. He gave her a quick kiss on the forehead before turning back to his car. "See'ya, Pen Pal," he called over his shoulder, and with that, he was gone, leaving Dan standing there, his hands clenched at his sides.

Christy looked back at Dan, her smile a little forced. "So, what's the story between you two?" Dan asked, trying to pretend he was only making conversation by placing the scanning plate into the suitcase, then zipping it up.

"Well, we date pretty often now and he's taking me to a reunion in two weeks. I guess it could get serious if that's what you want to know." She stated with no enthusiasm.

Dan could see the uncertainty in her eyes, the way she fidgeted. He wanted to say something—to tell her she deserved better, that Mark wasn't right for her. But the words stuck in his throat, his courage failing him once again.

He finished packing up the machine and decided it was time to leave. Before losing Christy to someone like Mark, he needed to act. He just needed more time. "well, I should get going," he said finally, forcing a smile. "I need to get this project sorted. I'll let you know how it turns out, okay?"

"I can go with you if you want some help," she offered as he rolled his window down.

"No, I have a lot of programming to do, and that could get pretty boring," Dan exaggerated, starting his engine.

"Well, do you want to go get something to eat? Cause I'm starving," Christy shared. "I've been craving a hoagie all day." She admitted with a smile. Dan's heart pounded once more. As much as he wanted to stay, he knew leaving was the best option right now.

"No thanks, I ate before I came," Dan said, remembering the breakfast bar he had before his arrival. "I'll let you know how the project turns out. Say bye to your mom for me."

Christy looked up, her smile returning, though it didn't quite reach her eyes. "Okay. Let me know when you finish it. Maybe we can celebrate."

Dan nodded, "Yeah. Maybe." It was sweltering in the car, and he didn't want his equipment to melt all over his data. "I'll call you soon," Dan said as Christy walked back to see him off. He forced a smile, trying to hide his disappointment.

"I'd like that," she said, her eyes softening. "Drive safe, Danny."

Dan nodded, getting into his car. As he drove away, he glanced in the rearview mirror, watching Christy grow smaller and smaller until she was out of sight. He sighed, gripping the steering wheel tightly. Dan stopped quickly at a deli on the way home to purchase a couple of sandwiches and drinks, having onon the way home. He couldn't help but feel like he had to do something—something to prove to her, and maybe even to himself, that he was worthy of her. But for now, all he could do was hope that the duplicate would give him the answers he needed to win her over securely.

Chapter 9

A Tangled Connection

THOUGH DAN WAS EAGER to begin, a gnawing unease held him back. The weight of what he was about to do—duplicating a human—settled heavily on his shoulders. He ran his fingers through his hair, pacing the lab, questioning if he was ready to move forward. What if this version of Christy wasn't truly her? What if the duplication didn't work, resulting in just a warped version of the woman he loved? The thought made his stomach churn.

Trying to shake his nervousness, Dan took a shower, hoping the warmth would wash away the tension. As he let the water run over him, he thought of Christy—her smile, her laughter, the way she had looked at him that afternoon. If only he could muster the courage to pursue her like anyone else would. If only he could be straightforward with her. Deep down, he realized that his urge to replicate her stemmed from his fear of her ending up with someone else.

Back in the lab, the duplicator loomed in the dim light, waiting. Taking a deep breath, Dan forced himself forward. It was time. He stood at the console, his hand hovering over the button, fingers trembling. Mustering his courage, he pressed it. The machine hummed to life, lights flickering across the platform as Christy's form took shape. First, a blur, then her familiar outline, until finally, there she was—disoriented, but undeniably Christy.

As she blinked, looking around in confusion, Dan rushed forward, catching her as she stumbled. "Are you okay?" he asked, voice shaky with tension. Her gaze met his, a mixture of confusion and curiosity in her eyes.

"Wow," she murmured, blinking. "You weren't kidding about being disoriented, were you!? It's like... I'm somewhere else." She scrunched her face, as if trying to clear her thoughts.

Dan swallowed, trying to force the words out smoothly. "You're okay," he reassured her, giving her a hesitant smile. Dan helped her down from the platform, his heart racing. The fear in her eyes mirrored the anxiety he felt. "You're in my lab," he said, striving to keep his voice calm. "It's alright, Christy, you're safe here," he reassured her with a cautious smile. "This is my, uh, home laboratory."

He offered his hand, which trembled a bit, ready to catch her if she stumbled. She gripped his hand tightly, and he could feel the anxiety in her touch, her eyes continuing to explore her surroundings. "How did we get here? And... how did you change your clothes so fast?" she asked, turning her attention back to him. Dan felt a jolt as her gaze locked with his—those eyes held such an intense mix of confusion, curiosity, and maybe a hint of concern. But he reminded himself: this wasn't the real Christy, she was just a duplicate.

He cleared his throat, awkwardly shifting his weight. "Uh, well, y-you see, there's... there's something I need to explain," he began, nervously pushing his safety glasses up the bridge of his nose.

Christy's eyes scanned his face, her thoughts racing. She was smiling. Had he unknowingly created something even more extraordinary? Could the machine be a dimensional gateway, a time capsule, or perhaps a teleportation device? She twirled around excitedly, captivated by all the potential accidental discoveries they may have found together. How Thrilling!

Dan took a deep breath, trying to steady himself. "Y-you've been... duplicated," he said, forcing the words out. As soon as he said them, Christy froze, her curiosity on full display. Her eyes went wide, and her mouth dropped open, her expression shifting from surprise to disbelief. She seemed to stand there for what felt like a full minute, her lips parted as if she couldn't quite find the words.

"What!?" she finally breathed, her voice barely audible. Her arms wrapped around her body protectively, and her eyes flickered back to Dan, demanding an explanation.

Dan scratched the back of his neck, taking a step back. "It's... it's a matter duplicator. The 3D imaging machine is a matter duplicator. I used it to... well, to create a duplicate of you, well — Christy." He tried to clarify, "You are a double, a replication of Christy. Right now, there's... there's the original you out there—the real Christy. And then there's... well, you." He forced himself to look her in the eye, hoping she could somehow understand.

"You're... serious?" Christy whispered, her voice trembling. She shook her head slowly. "You're serious... aren't you!?"

Dan nodded solemnly, his heart heavy as he noticed fear and confusion on her face. A wave of guilt washed over him—he didn't want her to be frightened or feel as though she were anything less than real.

"When I scanned Christy—the, uh, the original Christy—it was close to noon," Dan continued, his voice growing steadier as he tried to help her make sense of things. "It's now after seven. You don't... remember anything since then, do you!?"

Christy slowly looked down at her watch, 12:15pm, her expression darkening as she read the time, then glancing at the clock over the safety room showing way after 7pm. Her lips tightened, and her eyes flicked back to Dan's. Her confusion seemed to only deepen as she tried to reconcile the situation. "But... but I was just outside. My mom was there... You could've... kidnapped me? But..."

Dan shook his head quickly, feeling his nerves beginning to fray. "No, no! It's not like that. I'd never... It's just that you're... you're not her. You're a copy," he tried to explain, his voice almost pleading. He wanted so badly for her to understand, to trust him.

Christy swallowed, her eyes shining with unshed tears. "Danny, you're scaring me," she whispered. Her voice cracked, and her body seemed to shrink in on itself as she wrapped her arms around her middle. "And I... I don't want to be scared of you."

Dan's heart felt like it had shattered. He took a hesitant step toward her, wanting to comfort her, but she stepped back, her eyes wide, filled with fear. Dan stopped, his hands falling limply to his sides. He tried to smile, but it felt forced and hollow.

"It's... it's okay," he murmured. "I know it sounds crazy, but it's the truth. I promise." He gave her a weak smile, hoping that somehow, she could believe him.

Christy shook her head, a tear slipping down her cheek. "I... I want to go home," she said, her voice cracking.

Dan hesitated, his heart sinking. "You... you are home. The real Christy—she's home. You're here, and... and this is your home now too," he whispered, trying to make her understand. He saw her lips quiver, her eyes beginning to glisten with tears. Overwhelmed by helplessness, he felt a sense of despair. He had done this to her, and now she was suffering.

"Why?" she whispered, her voice cracking with emotion. "Why did you do this?"

Dan took a deep breath, closing his eyes for a moment. "B-because... I care about you. More than... more than I care about anything else," he confessed, his voice trembling. "Losing you to Mark terrified me. I wanted to... I wanted to be sure that I knew how you felt, without... without risking our friendship."

Christy's eyes were wide as she looked at him, tears falling freely now. "You duplicated me... because you were scared?"

Dan nodded slowly, his eyes downcast. "It was cowardly, I know. And wrong," he admitted, his voice barely above a whisper. "I just... thought maybe if I knew how you felt, I could... I could win the real you. And then... we could de-duplicate you, and everything would go back to normal."

Christy stared at him for a long time, her breathing shaky. She looked at the floor, her lips tightening. Finally, she let out a long sigh. "This is... so much," she said, her voice cracking. "It's too much."

Dan felt the weight of his actions pressing down on him, guilt clawing at his chest. He glanced at the fridge, remembering what he had brought. "Listen," he said, trying to lift the heavy mood. "The original Christy... she said she was craving a hoagie after I, um, scanned her. So... so I figured you'd be craving one, too. I, um, I got one for you."

Christy blinked, her eyebrows rising in surprise. Dan rushed over to the fridge, pulling out the paper bag and soft drink he had bought earlier. He handed them to her, his hands shivering.

Christy stared at the bag for a moment before her lips curved into a small, shaky smile. She took it from him, her eyes meeting his. "You really are something, you know that?" she said, her voice wavering as she took a bite of the hoagie.

Dan smiled, his heart lifting slightly as he saw her relax, even if just a little. "You know, this doesn't have to be all bad," he whispered. "Think of it as... as a sleepover. We can hang out, just like we used to." He gave her a hesitant smile, and to his relief, she smiled back—even if just for a moment.

"Maybe," she whispered, her voice still heavy with emotion.

After a long silence, she asked, "Where are we, again?" Her eyes roamed the room, still taking in everything.

Dan's smile grew a little wider. "You remember Mount Scorpion?" he asked, his eyes lighting up. She nodded, a flicker of recognition in her eyes. "I had this house built here. We're in the underground lab."

Christy's eyes widened, and she let out a soft laugh. "Wow. I always knew you were clever, but this is... really something," she said, her gaze softening. She took another bite of the hoagie, her eyes meeting his. "I guess I'll stay for a bit... for now."

Dan felt his heart swell, relief washing over him. He gestured toward the rabbits in the corner. "See those guys? The one with the dot is a duplicate too," he said, his voice tinged with pride.

Christy looked at the rabbits, her eyes lighting up. "They're cute. I guess... if they can get along, maybe I can too," she said, her lips curving into a small smile.

Dan felt warmth spread through his chest. "Yeah," he whispered. "Maybe."

He led her to the small room he had prepared for her, explaining that she could rest if she wanted to. She nodded, though time wise it was still early for her. She had exhaustion written across her features. As she stepped into the room, she looked back at him, her eyes filled with a mix of emotions. "Goodnight, Danny," she whispered.

Dan hesitated, then nodded. "Goodnight... Christy," he said, his voice cracking slightly. He watched as she closed the door, his heart heavy.

Dan couldn't shake the feeling that he had crossed a line. That maybe this was a mistake, and that he had let his emotions get the best of him. But it was too late now. Christy was here, and he had to figure out what to do next.

He stood there for a moment, his hand on the doorknob, listening to the soft sound of her crying. He closed his eyes, feeling the weight of his actions press down on him. She was just a duplicate; he told himself—just a copy. But the sound of her sobs tore at him in a way he couldn't quite shake. He sighed, turning away and heading to his room.

She was only a duplicate. That was all. So why did it hurt so much to see her hurt, to hear her cry?

Chapter 10

Moments of Freedom

CHRISTY SAT UP SLOWLY, stretching her arms over her head as her eyes adjusted to the dim glow of the built-in nightlights. Their soft illumination pierced the thick shadows, revealing smooth walls and unfamiliar furniture. She blinked hard. This wasn't her bedroom. It was too still, too polished. Sterile. The silence pressed against her like static.

She remembered fragments of last night's conversation—Dan's soft but urgent voice telling her she was duplicated, that he had created something extraordinary. The words made little sense. They still didn't. "You're just a copy of the real, Christy. She's home and you're here. With me."

She wanted to believe him. She really did. But every cell in her body ached with confusion. If what he said was true, then... what was she? A double? A dream? An experiment? No! It couldn't be. She felt real. Her memories—her laughter, her pain, the way her heart raced now—it all had to mean something more than just replicated code. She wasn't some artificial version of a person. It couldn't be. She refused to be.

And yet... the way he looked at her, so full of guilt and longing—it unsettled her. Like he knew something she didn't, something that mattered. "What else didn't he tell me?"

She bit her lip, wishing it had all been a bizarre nightmare. Wishing she could still trust him like she had just yesterday. But now, doubt threaded itself through every thought. The surrounding room might have been quiet, but inside, her mind was thundering.

Sliding to the edge of the bed, her feet touched the cold floor, sending a shiver up her spine. Her fingers trembled slightly as she slipped on her shoes. Her instincts screamed, "get out!"

She crept toward the door, heart hammering, and peeked into the lab beyond. A faint light flickered from inside, casting an eerie blue glow through the crack. Her breath caught. She scanned for movement—nothing. No sign of Dan. Just the hum of machines and the low flicker of monitors.

Keeping to the walls, she tiptoed through the lab, eyes darting toward strange devices and cables snaking across the floor. The duplicator stood still ominously in the corner. Cold. Waiting.

She spotted the elevator panel and pressed the button—once, twice, then again and again. No response. Her breath grew shallower, panic tapping at her edges. Swallowing hard, she turned and spotted a green-lit exit sign above a steel door. Hope surged. She rushed over, hand closing around the handle. A click. The door swung open easily, causing her to nearly lose her balance from using too much force. Spiral stairs curved upward into darkness.

She climbed quickly but carefully, every creak of the metal stairs echoing like thunder in her ears. At the top, a panel waited with a glowing blue button. She pressed it. A closet door swung open.

She stepped in—and froze. A shadow loomed behind her. Her heart leapt into her throat—but it was just her reflection, caught in the mirror at the back of the closet. She let out a shaky laugh, barely more than a whisper, and pressed on.

She emerged into Dan's bedroom. There he lay, sprawled across the bed with a hot water bottle resting on his head, unconscious or asleep. His breathing was steady. Peaceful. Too peaceful. In the pale morning light, he looked human—almost gentle. Her steps slowed.

Something pulled at her. She took a step toward him, her hand lifting on instinct... but she stopped herself just before touching his arm. Her breath hitched. No. Not now.

Silently, she slipped out, gently making her way downstairs. The hallway clock read 5:42 a.m. Her pulse echoed in her ears. She was almost free.

She moved through the kitchen, fingers brushing the counter, but just as she reached the front door, her elbow knocked over a small glass trinket. It shattered on the floor. The crash cut through the silence like a gunshot.

She froze. Every instinct screamed to run, to bolt out the front door—but her eyes caught something else. The house phone. Sitting on the counter. A direct line to the outside. To Tina. To home.

Her fingers were dialing before her brain caught up. Each beep of the numbers sounded impossibly loud. She didn't know exactly what she would say—but she knew she couldn't stay. Not another second.

Something clattered to the floor, breaking the silence. The sound seemed to echo. Dan's eyes shot open, heart racing. He scrambled downstairs, arriving to see Christy pale and frozen, phone in hand. His stomach dropped as he rushed forward, snatching the phone from her grasp and hanging up.

"Who did you call?" he demanded after securing the phone, his voice taut with desperation.

Her vacant stare slowly shifted, recognition dawning in her eyes.

"Home," she whispered, a tear slipping down her cheek.

Dan felt the world spin. "Damn," he muttered, running his hand through his hair, his other hand gripping his side. He turned away, trying to regain his composure. When he looked back at her, his face was full of urgency. "Who answered, Christy? Who picked up the phone?"

Christy swallowed hard, her face crumbling as tears rolled down her cheeks. "I did!." she whispered, her voice cracking. She looked down, her shoulders trembling. "I was there. I answered. It was me!" The weight of her realization hit her all over again. She broke into a sob, her whole body shaking as she clutched Dan's shirt. Dan's frustration vanished, replaced with guilt and remorse. He knew this was impossible for her to fully grasp—this new reality, the truth of her existence. It was too much for anyone. He let her cry, his arms holding her as she let out her grief.

Dan finally guided Christy over to the couch, sitting her down gently. He sat beside her, watching as she buried her head between her knees, her arms wrapped tightly around herself. Trying to reassure her, he softly explained himself again. He explained why he had duplicated her, the fears that had driven him to it, the hope that maybe, just maybe, it would lead to something beautiful. He spoke carefully, his words full of honesty, but also full of hope.

Christy stayed silent for a long time, listening. She lifted her head, her eyes red from crying. "You're pathetic," she finally said, her voice hollow.

Dan blinked, taken aback by the harshness of her words. "What!?" he asked, his heart sinking.

"You're pathetic. " She repeated, her gaze locking onto his. "You're brilliant, but you've done something so foolish, so wrong." She shook her head slowly, a sad smile crossing her lips. "You went through all of this just for me? Or, I guess, for her." She laughed bitterly. Then after a brief pause, "Okay, let's get started then. What do you want to know?" She insisted. Dan sat down on the loveseat and tried to think of any question, but nothing came to mind. She raised her eyebrow, looked straight at him, and waited. At a loss for words, Dan opened his mouth, only to close it. A frown appeared on his face, unable to think of anything.

"... How about," he yelled out as he thought of something, "What could I do to make Christy fall madly in love with me?" He asked with a hopeful glint in his eyes, looking at her expectantly. But Christy's duplicate was dumbfounded. She looked at him with a look of surprise, eyes wide open.

"Are you serious?" She shot. Dan gave a slightly nervous smile and shrugged his shoulders. "How am I supposed to know that!? I don't know. That's your job to figure it out." She combed her fingers through the ends of her hair. She raised her eyebrows. "You mean, you brilliantly thought out the entire detailed process of creating a duplicating machine. Then you thought of how to persuade me," she paused, then corrected herself, "I mean, her, who trusted you by the way, to stand on your duplicator apparatus thingamajig and pose for you so that you can ask the dupe, me, questions on what you could do to make her fall madly in love with you!?" She placed a hand on her lips, waiting expectantly for his answer. She noticed Dan's eyebrows knitting together, causing her to groan. Throwing herself back against the couch, she sighed, waiting. Dan looked frozen, deep in thought, contemplating on what the next step should be. Christy's voice broke the silence, soft but edged with something he couldn't quite name. She wasn't yelling. She wasn't crying. That almost made it worse. "I mean," she said, shifting her weight, not quite meeting his eyes, "if you intended to make a duplicate and run away with her... that would almost have a bit of romantic logic to it, I guess." Her words hung in the air, like a test—part accusation, part question. Dan didn't speak right away. He wasn't sure if she was joking, trying to make sense of it all, or barely holding something together. Christy continued before he could respond, her voice low but gaining strength with every word. "I mean, yeah, it'd be insane, obviously—but at least it would've meant you knew what you were doing. Like you had a plan. Like there was love behind the madness. But this?" She finally looked up at him, her eyes locked onto his. "You weren't even sure. You said it yourself—it was just an idea, a test. And I was... what? A guess?" Dan opened his mouth, but nothing came out.

She didn't wait for him to speak. "But to destroy or de-duplicate me—" her voice caught for a second, remembering his words last night, before she forced herself to keep going, "—and then go run off with her, the original, who would never even know any of this happened? Who'd never know about this insane act of love?" She gave a bitter laugh and crossed her arms. "It just sounds so... anticlimactic."

Dan's jaw tightened. He drew his shoulders inward and clasped his hands tightly in his lap, as if trying to disappear. He stared at the floor, unable to meet her gaze, realizing how small his brilliant idea had become under her scrutiny. Christy shook her head, more hurt than angry now. "You should never tell her, by the way. Ever. She doesn't need to carry this." Dan sat frozen, wide-eyed, stunned by how fast she had unraveled everything—his logic, his confidence, his plan. "In the end," she said, voice shaking just slightly, "you didn't create me because you were brave. Fear motivated you to do it. You didn't want to risk messing things up with her, so you tried to practice on me." Her arms tightened across her chest. "It's insane!" she finally burst out. "All of it." The silence that followed was heavier than before, filling the space between them like gravity.

Dan felt a mix of emotions—hurt, confusion, embarrassment. He wanted to defend himself, to explain again, but he found himself at a loss for words. Christy continued, her eyes narrowing. "You went through all this trouble, creating this ingenious machine and you didn't even think through what you wanted to ask me? You made me, and now you don't even know what to do with me." Dan opened his mouth to respond, but nothing came out. She was right. He hadn't thought beyond the duplication itself. He'd just assumed everything would fall into place, that somehow, this would answer all his questions.

Christy let out a sigh, her anger softening into something closer to pity. "You know, Danny, I know one thing," she said, her voice a little gentler. "The real me—she likes you. She really does. More than she likes Mark. But you always got so nervous, so awkward around her. You need to be confident. She likes you when you're confident."

Dan sensed something beyond her gentle smile, a certain look she had, and it made his heart flutter with a glimmer of hope. "How can I be more confident?" he asked, almost desperately.

Christy offered him a small, weary smile, her lips curving gently as her eyes shimmered with understanding. "Just be yourself, like you are right now. You haven't stuttered once." She paused momentarily, her gaze softening like the sun breaking through a cloudy sky. "That's because you think I'm just a stand-in, right? So, there's no risk. But you need to trust her, the real Christy, just like you're trusting me now." Dan nodded slowly, the weight of her words settling into his mind like pebbles sinking into a still pond. "So, is that it? I guess you could un-duplicate me now," she teased, half-jokingly.

There was a subtle click in Dan's mind, like a lock falling into place. His shoulders eased, and a soft exhale left him—almost like a sigh of relief. As he turned to Christy, his face softened, and a small grin tugged at the corners of his lips. His posture straightened, making him appear taller, steadier. A quiet spark lit up in his eyes—part excitement, part hope. He looked at her with a newfound confidence that seemed to radiate from within. "I'm hungry," he said, his voice light and inviting, "want to grab breakfast with me?"

Christy's eyes widened in surprise. "Go out? Really? You mean I'm not a prisoner?" she teased, her voice laced with playful disbelief. A smile tugged at her lips, half-curious, half-daring.

Dan chuckled softly, the sound easing between them. "Well," he said, with a shrug and a flicker of adventure in his tone, "as long as you're with me, yeah—we'll go someplace far away. Somewhere no one knows us."

Christy tilted her head, studying him. Her brows drew together ever so slightly in a moment of thought, as if weighing something deeper beneath the offer. Then, just as quickly, her expression shifted into something lighter, Dan watching her closely, captivated. "You know, that's not a bad idea," she exclaimed. "We could hang out," she added casually, "just for a few days or so." Her tone was breezy, but her eyes gleamed with intent. "Why not?" she shrugged, "That should be enough time for you to get comfortable around me..." Dan caught the glint in her eyes—clever, sharp, and knowing. She was baiting him, gently coaxing him toward a realization she already suspected he was circling. "After all," she added, her tone dropping just a touch, "I'm still Christy, right?"

Dan blinked, surprised. He hadn't quite seen it that way before—at least not so clearly. Yet now it was unmistakable and eye-opening. Spending time with Christy wasn't just comforting; it felt essential. Perhaps even unavoidable. It wasn't about controlling the situation or handling everything by himself anymore. It was about trust, about forming a connection. She wasn't asking for commitments, just his presence.

A new realization dawned on him, like a fog lifting from the landscape. The logic behind her idea struck him not with a jolt, but with clarity. Perhaps it didn't have to be so complicated. Maybe what he needed was already right in front of him, smiling.

Dan couldn't help but grin. "I'll think it over," he said with a playful air of mock-seriousness, then added, "Let's discuss it over breakfast."

He paused, his grin widening. "And to help minimize confusion going forward... let's call her Chris. And you—Christy."

Christy laughed, soft and full of light. She nodded in agreement, her smile radiant and genuine. "Deal," she said.

And just like that, the air between them changed—lighter, clearer, charged with the possibility that only comes when two people see each other as something more than circumstance.

Chapter 11

A Day in the Life That Could Be

BEFORE HEADING UPSTAIRS TO get dressed, Dan showed her the downstairs guest bedroom and bathroom, and where the new toothbrushes were. When he returned, Christy was waiting for him on the couch.

"You know, if you decide to keep me around for a few days, I'm going to need some clean clothes and... well, some undergarments too," she said, following him towards the side door leading to the garage.

"We'll stop by after breakfast and pick up a few things for you," Dan replied, his tone casual. He paused, then added, "I thought we'd drive towards Vegas. Do you know anyone there?" Christy shook her head, letting out a big smile.

They drove, the car filled with the soothing rhythm of wheels on asphalt. Laughter filled the air as they reminisced about old times. With a natural grace, words danced between them like leaves caught in a gentle breeze. Their dialogue shifted seamlessly, moving from one topic to another with ease. Christy looked at him admiringly from time to time, her smile broadening as she noticed how relaxed he was, how he spoke without a single stutter or hint of clumsiness. Her gaze lingered, warm and approving.

Eventually, they stumbled upon a cozy little restaurant nestled by the roadside. As they stepped inside, they chuckled at how quickly time seemed to have slipped by before settling down to order breakfast.

The aroma of freshly brewed coffee and sizzling bacon enveloped them. Dan observed her closely, intrigued by her habits—Her eyes moved swiftly and thoughtfully over the menu, and she selected her dish with such precision, as though each choice carried a hidden importance. As she ate, he noticed the delicate way she held her fork, the way she savored each bite, lost in her own world of flavors. He smiled to himself, thoroughly captivated by her little quirks that seemed to paint a vivid picture of her personality.

They chatted about her likes and dislikes. "Let's order champagne with orange juice to celebrate our well-thought-out plan," Dan suggested with a grin.

Christy gave him a sarcastic look, her lips curving into a smile. "I love the bubbles, but I'd rather have sparkling grape juice," she said with a laugh. "Sparkling grape juice is my favorite."

Breakfast made things feel more casual, almost normal, as they continued to share stories from their childhood, deepening the connection between them.

After breakfast, they drove around, searching for a clothing store. Christy turned to Dan, "I know this place—there's a clothing store two blocks from here. I came here once looking for a dress for the reunion. You'll never guess where I finally found it—K-Mart. After all that driving around!" They both laughed as they pulled up to the store.

"Do you mind waiting here?" Christy asked, her voice tinged with a hint of embarrassment. "I just need to grab a few personal items."

Dan handed her some money, and she disappeared inside. He waited in the car, time ticking by. After some time had passed, noticed folks going into the store then those folks leaving. He couldn't help but wonder—what if she left? What if she tried to escape? No, he thought, shaking his head, reassuring himself. Where could she go? She knew her situation. Still, the thought made him uneasy. He reached for the door handle, but before he could open it, he saw her exit the store, her arms full of bags.

He sighed in relief, a smile spreading across his face. She climbed into the car, placing the bags on the back seat. "Wow, six bags? You're only staying a few days, I thought," Dan teased, unaware of the gravity behind those words. Christy's expression faltered, a flicker of sadness crossing her face as she realized that her brief stay meant she would soon be deduplicated. He'd have to undo the duplication and she would cease to exist. Yet, her bravery shone through, and she quickly replaced the somberness with a bright smile.

"A girl needs all this." She insisted, "I bought a little makeup, underwear, a few pairs of shoes, some pants, a couple of skirts..." then handed him a twenty-dollar bill. "Here's your change."

Dan looked at her in surprise. "You spent three hundred and thirty dollars in a few minutes?" Dan playfully exaggerated.

Christy grinned mischievously and shrugged. "If you hand a girl money and tell her to go shopping, she's going to go shopping, and use every last cent if possible. Plus, there was an enormous sale going on." Both of them smiled as they drove away and eventually noticed a carnival, its lights shining vividly against the afternoon sky. They exchanged a grin and, without saying anything, Dan steered the car toward the entrance.

The carnival seemed to stretch out endlessly, with a vibrant complexity of roller coasters twisting and turning, games that beckoned with flashing lights, and stands overflowing with tantalizing treats and colorful trinkets. Laughter bubbled up between them as they soared on thrilling rides, captured playful moments in goofy snapshots, and tried their luck at various games. Christy won a plush stuffed animal and, with a beaming smile, handed it over to Dan, who accepted it with a mock flourish.

As the golden hues of day faded into the starry night, the temperature dropped, leading them to buy warm clothing—a comfortable sweater for her and a durable jacket for him.

The colorful lights of the carnival lit up the night sky, casting a dreamy glow over the bustling fairgrounds. Rides spun and whirled in a blur of neon, accompanied by the gleeful screams of thrill-seekers and the infectious laughter of children. Vibrant game booths lined the paths, their flashing lights and bold signage daring passersby to test their luck. The sweet scent of cotton candy and sugary funnel cakes mingled with the smoky aroma of grilled meats, hot dogs, and the earthy hint of hay drifting in from the nearby petting zoo. Even the occasional scent of gasoline from the roaring rides added an edge of thrill to the atmosphere.

Despite it all, Dan and Christy walked in quiet harmony, their fingers laced and steps in sync. Christy's head would rest against Dan's shoulder now and then, her body leaning into his as they strolled through the crowd. The soft murmur of their conversation blended with the surrounding clamor, cocooning them in a private moment within the chaos. There was a rhythm to it all—the lights, the sounds, the scents—each element enhancing the sense of warmth and connection between them as the world spun on in brilliant color around them. Their leisurely stroll led them past a booth displaying custom picture mugs and shirts. "Look, check this out," Dan exclaimed, pointing with excitement. "They had one of these in front of the market back in town." Christy glanced at the booth.

"Hey!," she said excitedly with an idea, "we could take the picture and give it to Chris and say it's the one you did. From the 3D machine of yours." They laughed, and she sat down and posed four different poses, then four more for a shirt. They picked the best two and had one picture placed on the mug and the other on the shirt.

They strolled around and Dan bought tickets to a hoop game. Christy threw the basketball, which hit the hoop and bounced back, hitting Dan on the head. Dan's look of surprise made them both laugh.

During dinner at an upscale, intimate restaurant, they chuckled about the underwhelming meal. While it didn't live up to its cost, the enjoyable company more than compensated for it. On the drive back, a comfortable silence filled the car as Christy nodded off in the passenger seat. Dan occasionally glanced her way, smiling gently, still in awe that she was truly there with him.

Even though she was a duplicate, it felt right—comforting—to have her there. He couldn't help but imagine what it might be like with Chris, the real Christy. But for now, this was undeniably invaluable practice.

When they arrived home, they unpacked the car together. They were both exhausted and barely managed a smile at one another while Christy went into the guest room, and Dan headed upstairs, exhaustion setting in. It had been a good day—maybe even the beginning of something better.

Chapter 12

Preparations and Realizations

THAT MORNING, DAN WOKE up to the warm smell of breakfast drifting through the house. He blinked his eyes open and sat up, realizing that Christy—well, her duplicate—must have made something. As he walked to the kitchen, he saw her standing by the stove, plates filled with golden French toast, a jug of fresh orange juice, and an assortment of colorful sliced fruits already laid out on the table.

"Good morning, sleepyhead," Christy said, her voice cheerful. Dan gave her a sleepy smile as he took a seat, his stomach rumbling at the sight of the food. Without wasting another second, Dan grabbed a fork and started eating. The first bite of the French toast made him close his eyes with delight.

"It's been so long since I've had French toast this good," Dan mumbled with his mouth full, glancing up at Christy with a grateful smile. She grinned, watching as he enjoyed his breakfast. "Where did you learn to cook so well?" Dan asked, genuinely curious.

Christy shrugged with a flair, flipping her hair with a playful edge. "I guess I've always had a knack for picking things up," she said, her laughter ringing like a bell. Dan joined in with a hearty chuckle, savoring another huge bite.

Dan looked up, his eyes locking with hers. "You know," he said, swallowing his mouthful with a grin, "if things go well with Chris, I could eat this kind of breakfast all the time."

Christy's smile wavered, a shadow crossing her face as reality's sharp edge cut through. She straightened, forcing a smile back onto her lips. "I think it's going to work out just fine... for you and her," she said softly, her voice tinged with an unmistakable sadness. She rose, gathering the dishes with deliberate movements, and carried them over to the sink, leaving behind a heavy silence.

Dan watched her for a moment before deciding to head down to the lab to tend to the rabbit. He adjusted the duplicator to be ready for de-duplication. For both of them, he wanted to ensure a painless process. He was about to run a few tests, but decided to go back up with Christy. Christy was tidying up the kitchen when he found her. He cleared his throat, making sure not to startle her. "Hey, I was thinking about asking Chris out on a date sooner than later," Dan started, trying to sound casual. "I want it to be perfect, and I was hoping you could help me plan it."

Christy looked at him, her eyes softening. "You want my help?" she asked, tilting her head slightly. Dan nodded, and a smile slowly spread across her face. She walked over to him, grabbing a notebook off the counter. "Alright, then let's make this date amazing," she said, her voice full of determination.

Christy explained her idea of the perfect date—a picnic. She spoke with bright eyes and animated hands, describing every detail like she'd been planning it forever. A variety of small sandwiches, all cut just right, drinks in glass bottles, maybe even a checkered blanket. Dan's face lit up as he listened, her energy rubbing off on him like sunlight.

She even described the location, her voice softening with wonder. "I saw it in this documentary once," she said dreamily. "It's quiet... just outside the city. There's this patch of soft grass near a bend in the stream. The birds are always singing, and there are these low-hanging trees that cast the perfect shade." She paused, eyes unfocused for a second. "The way the mountains stood out in the background, it looked like... desert magic."

But as the image formed between them, Dan noticed her smile falter. It was slight, but it was there—the kind of sadness that crept in when someone remembers something they never really had. Her voice trailed off, and the glow in her face dimmed, like the dream had suddenly slipped from her hands. Maybe it was the way her fingers twisted together in her lap, or how she blinked a few times too quickly, but Dan could see it—deep down, she wasn't sure if the picnic wasn't truly hers to envision. It belonged to someone else... the real version of her.

Dan felt it, the quiet weight between them. He wanted to reach across it.

"You want to go with me to buy supplies for the picnic?" he asked gently.

Christy looked up, startled, then smiled. "Yeah. I'd like that."

The moment lifted. They both went to get ready, shaking off the haze of thoughts neither of them voiced out loud. Another casual adventure, Christy thought. Something to hold on to.

They drove just outside of town, windows down, letting the wind carry their worries. After picking up a new picnic blanket, plates, a basket and other picnic essentials, they wandered into a secondhand shop and picked out a couple of silly outdoor games and another picnic basket.

As they passed a small movie theater with vintage posters, Christy nudged him. "Want to see something dumb and funny?"

Dan grinned. "Only if we get popcorn." They both laughed, heading inside, ready to forget for a little while and just be. On the way home, they stopped at a small supermarket and picked up some drinks, items to make sandwiches, and other things for home-cooked meals.

The following morning, Dan had made his traditional breakfast he often made for himself: fried eggs, hash browns, bread and bacon. "It's cute seeing you in an apron." Christy said and smiled, then poured out a large glass of orange juice for both of them. "It looks delicious." She added, grabbing some toast to butter them.

While sitting there, Dan pointed at two picnic baskets he had set out earlier. "Which one do you think is better—the dark brown or the pale brown?" he asked.

Christy studied the baskets for a moment before pointing to the dark one. Christy looked at him, her smile wavering. She took a deep breath, trying to steady her emotions. "I wish it was me going on the date with you," she admitted, her voice barely a whisper. Dan swallowed hard, feeling the weight of her words.

"You kind of are," he said, trying to lighten the topic. But Christy shook her head, forcing a smile.

"No," she said softly. "I mean, — I wish I was Chris, the original one. It would be so much fun if it were really me." a bittersweet smile tugging at her lips.

Christy barely finished her breakfast and stood up. She opened the refrigerator and started gathering items for the picnic. "Cold cuts are the best choice, I think," she said, her voice livelier now, "because they're easy to eat and non-messy! " She made a variety of small sandwiches cutting off the crust.

Dan watched her with admiration as she continued to plan everything, despite knowing she wouldn't be the one going on the date. He admired her strength. When she finally looked up at him, he gave her a small, appreciative smile. "You're amazing," he whispered. She smiled, though he could see the sadness lingering in her eyes. He cleaned up the kitchen and helped pack the basket, but she playfully chewed him off.

"You know," she said with a slight sigh, "this feels like cheating. You've got all the answers before the test. It hardly seems fair." She gave a small laugh, but her eyes looked distant.

Dan frowned, trying to explain. "I didn't want to risk losing her, or our friendship," he said.

"They're both so important to me, I didn't trust myself. — I only wanted to make sure it was perfect."

Christy shook her head gently. "Danny, you should have put your trust in her! You cheated! You Ought to call her right now and ask her to lunch. And don't mention the picnic! "

Dan hesitated, uncertainty creeping into his voice. "But what if she says no?"

"She won't!" Christy reassured him, "I wouldn't." Her smile was genuine this time. Dan took a deep breath, feeling a rush of courage. He picked up the phone, dialing Chris's number. He could hear her excitement on the other end, and his heart soared as he asked her out. After a few moments, he hung up and turned to Christy.

"She said yes. Saturday," he said, his smile wide. Christy jumped up, hugging him, her excitement contagious. "See? I told you," she said, her voice full of joy. Dan laughed, hugging her.

They continued packing, but a heaviness settled over the room as Dan spoke. "After the date, if all goes well, I guess I should... de-duplicate you." His words were hesitant, and Christy nodded, though the sadness in her eyes grew deeper. She carefully folded a checkered picnic blanket, placing it in the basket, her hands moving slowly, almost as if she wanted to prolong the moment.

Dan noticed her sudden quietness, and it made him shift uncomfortably. He couldn't help but feel a strange attachment to her, one he hadn't expected. He missed her voice, her presence, and he wasn't ready for this to end. "I have an idea," he blurted, his voice breaking the silence. "Since the date isn't until tomorrow, why don't we have a practice picnic today?"

Christy's eyes lit up, her smile returning. "That's a great idea!," she said eagerly. They packed another basket, filling it identical to the last one. "This will help us find the perfect spot," Christy added, her excitement making Dan's heart feel lighter.

They drove a few minutes outside the city, following Christy's directions until they found a small, quiet spot off-road, framed by a few sturdy trees and a gentle stream trickling nearby. The late afternoon sun bathed everything in a golden hue, making the scene feel like something out of a dream.

Christy hopped out of the car before it had even fully stopped, her eyes wide with excitement. "Look, there's the stream!" she called, her voice bubbling with delight as she twirled on the grassy patch. Her laughter carried on the breeze, light and carefree, making Dan shake his head with an amused smile.

"You're acting like you've never seen water before," he teased, stepping out and stretching his arms.

She spun back to face him, hands on her hips. "Excuse me, but this is perfect picnic scenery. It's basically required that I be excited."

Dan chuckled as they found the perfect spot near the water and set up their blanket. Christy plopped down, practically bouncing as she opened the picnic basket and handed him a sandwich. "Part of the fun is not knowing what kind you get," she said with a mischievous grin.

Dan took a bite, chewing thoughtfully before raising a brow. "Mystery sandwich, huh? What if I got something awful?"

"Then you suffer in silence," she declared, taking a dramatic bite of her own.

His lips quirked up. "And here I thought you were nice."

Winking, she said, "Nice is overrated."

As they ate, Christy's eyes flickered over the picnic basket, landing on a bottle of sparkling grape juice and two plastic champagne glasses. Her smile softened as she carefully lifted them out, a look of wonder flashing across her face.

"You remembered!... from that night," she murmured, looking up at him almost in awe.

Dan gave a small shrug, grabbing another sandwich. "Of course I did."

She studied him for a little while, something unreadable in her expression. Then, with a sudden grin, she nudged his knee with hers. "You should definitely do this for Chris."

After they ate, they spent the afternoon exploring the stream, skipping stones, and splashing water at each other in a playful battle that quickly escalated. Christy, determined to get the upper hand, flicked water at Dan's face before dashing away in a fit of giggles.

"Oh, you're in trouble now," Dan warned, chasing after her.

She yelped as he lunged, but just as she dodged, his foot hit a slippery rock, and—with an undignified yelp—he tumbled straight into the stream. The splash was spectacular.

For a few seconds, Christy was silent. Then she doubled over laughing, clutching her sides as tears sprang to her eyes. "Oh, my—oh no, you okay?" she gasped between giggles.

Dan sat up, dripping and unamused. "Yeah, yeah. Laugh it up."

But he couldn't help the slow grin spreading across his face. With a sudden move, he grabbed her hand and pulled her forward. "No—wait, Dan—!" she squeaked as she lost her footing and tumbled right into the water with him. Now they were both soaked, sitting in the shallow stream, their laughter echoing through the trees. "Okay," she huffed, wiping her face. "Maybe I deserved that."

Dan smirked. "You definitely deserved that."

Later, as the sun dipped lower, they sat side by side on the picnic blanket, their damp clothes slowly drying in the fading warmth of the day. The sky melted into shades of orange and pink, a quiet hush settling over them.

"Mmmm, smells like rain," Christy murmured, leaning her head on Dan's shoulder. Her gaze drifted toward the distant horizon where dark clouds rolled in, her eyes glistening with something unreadable. "I wish this moment could last forever."

Dan stared at the sky, something heavy settling in his chest. "I know," he whispered. A pause. Then, almost too soft to hear, he added, "I wish you were the real her, too."

Christy inhaled sharply, her entire body tensing. Slowly, she lifted her head to look at him, searching his face as though willing him to take the words back.

"I am her," she whispered, voice trembling. "Aren't I? I'm here... right now, with you."

Her fingers brushed against his cheek, tentative, desperate. Dan swallowed hard, his mind at war with his heart. He shouldn't feel this way—he couldn't. She was only a replica. But when he gazed at her, something inside him crumbled.

Without thinking, he leaned in, pressing his lips softly against hers.

It was barely more than a whisper of a kiss, but it sent a shiver through them both. When they pulled away, neither spoke. They just sat there, caught in a moment that felt too fragile to break.

Christy closed her eyes, her heart pounding in anticipation.

Finally, Dan exhaled and glanced at the darkening sky. "We should go before it gets too dark."

They stood, shaking out the blanket and packing up, but just before they finished, Dan turned to her again.

This time, when he kissed her, it was real. It was deeper, lingering. When they finally pulled apart, he pulled her into a long, tight embrace.

"Thanks for a perfect day," he murmured.

Her smile, the way she looked at him—it made him feel whole and shattered all at once. He kept repeating to himself, She's only a duplicate. She's not real. But if that were true, then why did she feel so achingly, impossibly real?

Letting go, he forced a smile. "I can't wait to do this for real with Chris tomorrow."

Christy flinched, just barely, but covered it with a small laugh.

They hurried to clean up as darkness crept in. Dan took a final deep breath before opening the car door for her.

"I love the smell of distant rain," he said, smiling as he looked up at the sky.

Then he shut the door, sealing the moment away.

The way home started off with joyous laughter as they recounted the highlights of the day—the ridiculous sandwich mystery, Dan's epic fall into the stream, and the way Christy had squealed when he pulled her in after him. Their voices were light, teasing, filled with an easy warmth that neither wanted to let go of just yet.

But as the miles stretched on, the conversation faded. Silence settled over them—not the awkward kind, but the kind that wrapped around them like a soft blanket. Lost in their own thoughts, they replayed the evening's final moments. Content. Euphoric. And yet, beneath the glow of happiness, there was something else. Something unspoken.

By the time they pulled into the driveway, the night had deepened, the scent of distant rain still lingering in the air. They moved in sync, unpacking the car together with no need to speak, their movements practiced and familiar.

Dan stretched, rolling his shoulders. "We ought to get out of these sticky clothes," he said, breaking the silence. "I'll throw them in the wash when you're ready."

Christy gave a small shake of her head, gathering up the towels and a few other items. "I'll do it," she insisted, a touch too quickly.

Dan raised a brow, amused. "You sure?"

"Yep! Just throw yours down," she called over her shoulder, heading toward the laundry room. The truth was, she had a few things of her own she wanted to toss in, and she wasn't exactly keen on Dan seeing certain items of hers mixed in with his. The thought made her cheeks warm.

Upstairs, Dan chuckled to himself before peeling off his damp clothes and tossing them over the railing. He could hear Christy moving around downstairs, the hum of the washer starting up.

Stepping into the shower, he let out a deep sigh as the warm water cascaded over his head. The heat was soothing, washing away the chill that had crept into his skin after their impromptu swim in the stream. He leaned his head against the tile, letting the events of the day replay in his mind. The way Christy had looked at him. The way she had felt in his arms. Between reality and the impossible, his heart had wavered.

With a shake of his head, he turned off the water, grabbed a towel, and filled up his hot water bottle, placing it near his pillow.

Descending the stairs, he had the sudden thought Christy might want some hot cocoa before bed. He made his way toward the laundry room, but as he reached the doorway, he paused.

Christy had curled up on the couch, her legs tucked beneath her, a towel wrapped snugly around her damp hair. Her breathing was slow and steady, her face peaceful in sleep.

Dan glanced at the washing machine. She had set it to pre-soak, extra wash, and an extended rinse—a setting that would take a while, buying her enough time to rest before moving the clothes to the dryer. Thoughtful, as always. She had even left the door open slightly, likely to hear the cycle alarm to ring high when finished. A small smile tugged at his lips. She always thinks ahead.

He considered waking her, but instead, he simply grabbed the knitted throw from the back of the couch and draped it over her shoulders. For a moment, he just stood there, watching her.

Then, with a soft sigh, he turned and made his way upstairs.

Slipping into bed, he pressed his hand lightly against the warmth of the hot water bottle laying on his head, letting his eyes drift toward the ceiling. The air smelled faintly of rain, clean clothes, and something else—something familiar. Something surprising her.

And as he closed his eyes, one thought lingered in his mind, refusing to fade.

She's only a duplicate. Then why did she feel so real?

Chapter 13

Sincere Apologies

Dan woke up hungry, and for a moment, he had hoped to smell one of Christy's delicious breakfasts wafting through the house. But the air was still, and the events of the previous night weighed heavily on him. Dan rubbed his forehead in exasperation before getting up, heading downstairs in search of something to eat.

As he reached the bottom of the stairs, Dan paused, noticing his clothes neatly folded on the bottom step. Christy was there in the kitchen, setting up the table. She had made cream of wheat, with toast and butter, all neatly laid out. She looked up and smiled.

"Hey, good morning," Dan said, genuinely surprised.

"Good morning," Christy replied warmly, her voice as comforting as ever. "I thought a warm breakfast would be nice, considering it rained all night."

Dan smiled back, a genuine gleam reaching his eyes as he peered into the pot. "It looks great, thanks," he said, his voice trailing off into a pensive silence. A complicated swirl of feelings wrestled within him, and he took a deep breath, trying to steady the mental turmoil. "You know, I truly am sorry... for all of this." The words left him in a rush, and he paused, biting his lip as his eyes wandered down to the breakfast. The effort Christy had put into it made his chest tighten with guilt and appreciation. His heart pounded loudly, echoing in his ears, as he added, "This whole wacky idea," nearly swallowing the last words.

An overwhelming impulse surged through him, and without thinking, he turned towards her, pulling her into a spontaneous hug.

Christy stiffened momentarily, surprise flashing across her features, but then she melted into the embrace, her form softening against him. Dan embraced her softly, almost cautiously, as if worried she might disappear. His voice dropped to a whisper, laced with earnest emotion. "You're wonderful!" he exclaimed, squeezing her a little tighter. "I shouldn't have put you through any of this!" The words carried the weight of his regret.

Dan's voice trembled with vulnerability, an admission of the truth he had long avoided. Despite her being a duplicate, everything he had put her through—the confusion, the hope, the uncertainty—crashed down around him in a wave of emotion. His heart raced as he held her, acknowledging her role in this tangled web they had woven. It was a confession layered with remorse, yet filled with a raw honesty that he had never dared to express until now. He hugged her more tightly, the enormity of his actions and their repercussions nearly overwhelming him. An apology not just for the last few days but for the entangled mess of feelings and decisions that had led them here. Christy said nothing, but the way she leaned into him spoke volumes, her body language offering a reassuring acceptance. Dan closed his eyes, trying to capture the moment, grateful for her forgiveness and the unexpected comfort it brought.

He could feel the rhythm of her breathing, steady and calming, and it soothed the roiling thoughts in his mind. A sense of calm replaced the frantic beating of his heart, and he wished he could stay like this, suspended in this fragile peace, for just a little while longer. Christy took a deep breath, her form rising and falling gently against him, and he wondered what she was thinking—how she could be so understanding, so... herself. The question lingered as he felt her hold on to him, just as he was holding on to her, both in the literal and more profound sense. Her presence was an anchor, and he marveled at how he had taken her for granted, expecting so much without fully appreciating the impact on her. For a moment, he feared she might pull away, but she stayed enveloped in the quiet intimacy they shared.

Christy closed her eyes and leaned into him, feeling the comfort of his warmth. "Thanks, Danny." She rested her head against his shoulder, holding him gently, almost as if she were savoring each moment of closeness. Her embrace was tender and cautious, a soft and hesitant grip—as if she feared that if she held on too tightly, it would make the inevitable letting go hurt even more. She lingered there, wrapped in the quiet intimacy of the moment, before pulling away and kissing him lightly on the cheek. "Come on, breakfast is ready," she said, her voice lighter, but carrying an undertone of emotion. She motioned towards the table, as if trying to shift the mood to something more carefree. "Besides, I'm having a good time. I don't have to worry about my mom, dad, or sisters." Her smile carried both warmth and complexity as she tried to make light of their unusual situation. "I mean, I'm still there taking care of them, right?" She attempted to laugh, though it sounded a little uncertain. Dan sat down at the table, his eyes on her, watching the way she moved with a mixture of familiarity and newfound appreciation.

She continued speaking, her tone an odd mix of cheerfulness and resignation. "It feels like a mini vacation. Not that I don't miss them, but..." She paused, perhaps searching for the right words, before looking at him with an openness that seemed to ask for understanding. "I've enjoyed my time with you, even though I know it's temporary." Dan returned her gaze with an almost foolish smile, his fingers absently toying with his spoon. There was relief in hearing that she was happy, but also a growing weight on his conscience as he thought of his plans for her. Christy sighed softly, a sound both contented and wistful, and glanced at him with an expression that mingled affection with something deeper. "You know," she began, her voice layered with sincerity, "I don't want to leave, even though I know she'll be here for you." She hesitated, her eyes searching his, as if trying to gauge his true feelings. "It feels like... I'm going to miss you, too." Dan's heart skipped a beat at her words, a mixture of joy and guilt stirring within him. To hear her say that meant more than he could express, but it also brought the reality of his decision crashing back down. Christy's voice sounded more fragile as she asked, "Do you think the de-duplication is going to hurt? I mean, you've never done this before."

Dan's smile flinched, and he forced himself to reply, hoping that the truth would offer little comfort. "If it does hurt, it'll be over in an instant," he said, struggling to sound reassuring. "You wouldn't even feel it." But even as he spoke, the thought gnawed at him, twisting inside his chest. He hated imagining her in pain, even for a fraction of a second. For so long, he had convinced himself that this was the best solution, the most logical outcome. Yet sitting there with her, the stark reality of his choice loomed larger than ever, and the thought of de-duplicating her now felt unbearably complex. She had become more than an extension of Christy; she was a part of his life, a part he now realized he couldn't so easily erase.

Christy looked at him, her eyes filled with uncertainty. "That's hardly comforting," she said with a half-hearted smile. She looked away, her voice breaking. "Not existing anymore... it's kind of like knowing I'm dying. Like going to the doctor's, getting an injection, and then... no more me. Not even knowing if I have a soul or not."

Dan sighed, his shoulders slumping. "I know! This was a horrible idea," he admitted, his voice raw with emotion. Every part of him felt the gravity of his choices, like an anchor pulling him into a sea of regret. He looked down at his hands, the same hands that had set all of this in motion, feeling their heaviness as if they held the entire burden of his failed plans. "I thought I was doing something brilliant," he continued, almost to himself, his words tinged with disbelief at his own foolishness. "But all I did was make things worse." He was stumbling through the confession, overwhelmed by the tangled mess he had created. It was as if speaking the words made them more real, and he struggled with the enormity of what he'd done. He could hardly bear to look at Christy, fearing he would see disappointment in her eyes. Instead, her gaze was steady, watching him with far more understanding than he believed he deserved.

Seeing Dan so vulnerable, Christy's heart ached with empathy. She leaned forward, trying to meet his downcast eyes. "Dan," she said gently, "you were just trying to guarantee... you wanted to be with me... well, her." Her voice was soft, infused with the kindness that came so naturally to her. She paused, searching for words that might comfort him, that might forgive him. "I know you didn't mean to hurt anyone," she added, her words wrapping around him like a warm embrace. She understood the complexity of his heart, perhaps even better than he did. Her compassion made Dan's confession feel both easier and harder; easier because she listened without judgment, and harder because it reminded him of how deeply he had entangled her in his hopes and desires.

"Instead, I hurt you," Dan replied, his voice quivering with a mix of regret and confusion. The look in her eyes was almost unbearable, but he could not tear his gaze away. "All of this," he gestured around them, trying to capture the chaos of the room, the house, their entire surreal predicament. "I never wanted—" His voice faltered, trapped between remorse and justification. She was supposed to be just a duplicate, a mere experiment. A safe way to navigate the uncertainties he couldn't face with the real Christy. It had all seemed so rational, so controlled, so perfectly sensible. He swallowed hard, grappling with the whirlpool of emotions threatening to drown him. The reality of his actions crashed over him, each wave leaving him more unsteady. He had told himself it was the right thing, the only way to achieve the life he envisioned. Yet now, as he sat there, the tangled mess of his choices suffocating him, he realized just how disastrously he had misjudged everything. "I'm so sorry!"

Christy tried to lighten the mood, her voice half-joking. "Hey, I have an idea. Why don't you make a duplicate of yourself? Then he and I can run away together. And you can duplicate my family. Oh, and Tina, too!"

Dan snorted, a smile breaking through his gloom. "Oh no, it sounded fine, but the idea of two Tina in the world? No way!"

They both laughed, and for a moment, the heaviness between them lifted. Christy shook her head. "She's not that bad. Besides, I wouldn't wish this on anyone. It's all so... mind-boggling. Part of me just wants it to be over, just so I don't have to think about it anymore!"

Dan nodded, his heart heavy. "If I could take it all back, I would. I'd break the machine. I wish I'd never built it... even though I learned so much, and even though I've had such an Amazing, time with you." He looked at her, his voice breaking. "I'm so sorry."

Christy placed her hand on his shoulder, her eyes kind. "Well, it's not over yet," she said, smiling faintly. "I checked the basket in the fridge. The sandwiches looked soggy, so I made some fresh ones. I'll take the old one for lunch. It'll be like I'm having lunch with you, even if just in spirit."

Dan nodded, forcing himself to smile. The thought of Christy's duplicate no longer being around weighed on him. He finished breakfast, thanked her, and then went downstairs to check on the batteries and tend to the rabbits. The complexity of the situation overwhelmed him. He imagined how much worse it could have been if Christy hadn't been so understanding and cooperative. He shook his head, a thought echoing in his mind—"She is so wonderful."

He needed to adjust the duplicator to be ready for de-duplication. For both of them, he wanted to ensure a painless process. He ran a few tests, starting with some fruits. After a few successful tries, Dan was confident enough to test it on a living subject, the duplicated rabbit.

The rabbit sat on the platform, unaware of what was happening as the de-duplication process began. Dan watched the monitor, his heart pounding as he saw the duplicate disassemble. It was over quickly, with no sign of distress. The rabbit's double vanished, and Dan let out a long sigh of relief. Everything had worked perfectly, but the thought of the rabbit being there one moment, alive, and gone the next, haunted him. His stomach twisted. He knew that soon, it would be Christy standing on that platform.

As the weight of the task loomed over him, he remembered something else—his date with Christy, the original. He glanced at the clock and gasped. "Oh no! My date! I'd better get going!"

He rushed upstairs, brushed his teeth, and shaved, trying to clear his mind of the doubts that lingered. Everything he needed was waiting for him by the door, so he hurried downstairs. He looked up and saw Christy standing there, her arms crossed, almost hurrying him with her eyes. Her expression was soft, but her eyes held a sadness that tugged at his heart.

He took a deep breath and confessed. "I wish it was you going with me," he admitted, feeling the weight of the moment.

"I kind of am," she exclaimed, smiling, remembering his words when he tried to lighten the topic the other day. "Don't be nervous," she said gently. "You'll do just fine. Just be yourself." She smiled, trying to reassure him. "And so what if you're a little late? Mark is always late, and she is still with him, right?"

Dan gave her a weak smile. "Yeah, which means you like him too, right!?" he said, trying to make light of the situation, but the words felt hollow. Something about this moment felt wrong. Why did he feel like he was cheating on her? On Christy, this version of her, the one here, by his side all along.

"Frankly," Christy said, her tone teasing, "I don't see what she sees in him anymore." She pretended to think hard, and Dan pretended to be shocked. They both laughed, but there was a hint of sadness behind their smiles.

Christy stepped closer to him, her smile fading. "I wish you the best, Dan. Don't forget, she'll love you. I'm sure... as much as I love you!" She placed her hand on his chest, leaning in to kiss him. Her touch was so gentle, her lips soft against his. Dan's mind went blank, and his heart seemed to stop, savoring the moment. Then, just as suddenly, she pulled away, and the warmth of her presence left him feeling cold.

"Go!" she urged, opening the door for him, her eyes bright but sad. Dan nodded, picking up the basket with the blanket tucked into the handles. He walked to his car, glancing back at her one last time as she leaned on the doorframe, watching him.

Chapter 14

The Date

THE DRIVE TO CHRIS'S house felt surreal. His thoughts kept drifting back to the kiss—how it felt, how real it had been. He remembered their practice picnic, the laughter, the connection. He wished he could turn the car around and go back to her.

He finally approached the door and paused on the walkway, his heart pounding. He saw the figure standing at the door—Chris. But for a heartbeat, just one breathless moment, it was Christy he saw. Not just a resemblance—no, it was the way she stood, the quiet tilt of her smile, the way her fingers tucked a strand of hair behind her ear.

It was familiar in a way that lifting his spirits.

She greeted him with a warm smile. "Hey, you! You look happy," she said, her eyes full of warmth. Dan was so glad to see her, but with the realization that she wasn't Christy, his smile felt forced.

"Hello, Danny," Linda said, popping out from behind the door. She handed Chris a thin coat. "Just in case it gets cold," she said with a smile. "No harm in being ready." Then she disappeared back inside, her voice drifting through the door as she tended to Kathy.

"This is going to be so much fun," Chris said, tapping her hands together with excitement. "I've been looking forward to this." Her joy radiated in a way that felt both familiar and new. And even though Dan knew this wasn't the Christy he had shared those recent memories with, something inside him softened.

"Where do you want to go? I still haven't had that hoagy if you want to go there?"

Dan turned to face her, his mind freezing for a moment. She looked so much like Christy. She is the real Christy, after all. He had to keep from talking about his recent experiences with Christy.

"No, though a sandwich doesn't sound bad," Dan said, looking down to hide the smirk that formed on his face as he opened the passenger door for her. So far, so good.

"I know this new pizza place that opened up not too far from here, and I know how much you like pizza," she said with her same remarkable smile as he got in on the driver's side. Her smile had a way of lighting up more than just her face—it lit something in him too.

He smiled slightly at the sight, shaking off the strange familiarity that clung to him like a shadow.

He started the car to begin their voyage. "Not bad," he said, glancing at her. "But I thought we could go someplace else."

"Okay, where?" Her voice perked with interest, the edge of curiosity creeping into her tone.

"I found this quiet spot near the edge of the city. It might take a while," he said, raising an eyebrow. "You game?"

"Yes! I like surprises!" she beamed, buckling her seatbelt. As he glanced at her again, something shifted in his chest. It was strange. Christy's smile reminded him of Chris—the one from the dream. Or maybe it was the other way around. Why wouldn't it? This wasn't her twin, but an exact double. An image of the departing kiss they had shared in that other life flickered across his mind, as vivid as if it had happened just yesterday.

She folded her hands in her lap, then added softly, "I'm just... glad to be here with you."

Dan glanced at her, offering a slight smile of encouragement.

There was a silence between them. Not uncomfortable—just... charged.

Chris eventually broke it with a chuckle. "So, tell me more about this secret pizza-alternative hideout. Am I going to need hiking boots?

Dan grinned, grateful for the shift. "Neither. You'll just have to wait."

She turned to face him, one hand on the edge of her seat. "Well," she started. "No matter where this day ends, I'm glad I said yes."

Dan swallowed the knot forming in his throat and focused on the road ahead. For once, he wasn't running from anything—not even himself.

Dan glanced at her encouragingly. "I'm so glad to be here with you. You seem different, good different, I mean. How's your science business in California going?" She asked, changing the subject.

Dan talked about work and how he would like for Steve to come to visit.

Her eyes sparkled with interest as she watched him speak. "You are different. You haven't stuttered once," she commented, nodding in agreement with the realization.

Just then, the windshield began roaring with the intense beat of rain. Dan looked up at the gloomy sky. "Where's that coming from? There are hardly any clouds." His eyebrows knitted together at the thought of the date getting canceled.

"Oh, I love the rain! Oh, look, it stopped," Chris added. It ended as fast as it had started. A comfortable silence fell between them as they looked at each other and smiled.

"So, how's... how's it going between you and Mark?" Dan asked after a while, looking back at the road.

"Oh, let's not talk about him. I'm so glad you're here." She looked back at the road, noticing they had turned onto a dirt pathway. "Is that it?" They were in the middle of what looked like nowhere.

When they finally arrived at the quiet clearing, framed by sturdy trees and a gentle, winding stream, the late afternoon sun painted everything in golden hues.

Chris stepped out, stretching before inhaling deeply. "Oh, wow, this is beautiful," she murmured, smiling. "I think I know this place." She looked up, taking in a deep breath, her arms out. "Smells wonderful here, like it rained. I bet it was that storm that briefly hit us on the way." The air felt humid, but she was too eager to let that bother her, it seemed. "Look, a rainbow," she pointed

"I thought we'd have a picnic here, right over there," he said, pointing to a group of trees to the right, feeling reminiscing. He cleared his throat, nodding at the familiar sight.

"Oh," she exclaimed softly, "A picnic, that's so perfect!" She proclaimed, "And look, there's a family over there. Come on, let's go to the stream." Her smile grew even more radiant than before. Dan was disappointed they would not be alone this time, but it didn't seem to bother her. "It's so beautiful here," she said, Dan following closely. "Look, let's cross here."

"Careful, that stone is slippery!" Dan grabbed her arm just as she landed on it, losing her balance. He quickly pulled her towards him before she could have fallen in.

"Whoa! My hero!" She gazed at him with these enormous eyes. Dan, with a concerned smile, gently placed Chris on her feet. She stood there momentarily, taking advantage of their embrace. "Um, let's go eat," she said, looking away. "I'm starving."

They spread the blanket together, but as a breeze picked up, Chris laughed, holding it down. The moment struck Dan with an unexpected pang of déjà vu—he had done this before, with another version of her. A version who had laughed just as freely. He pushed the thought away, forcing himself to focus on the present.

As they settled in, Chris reached into the picnic basket and gasped in delight as she pulled out a bottle of sparkling grape juice. "I love this stuff! How'd you know?"

Dan opened his mouth but hesitated.

Chris's excitement grew when she spotted the mug. She held it to her chest, her expression a mix of joy and nostalgia. "Oh my goodness, you remembered this!"

"Yeah," he said, his voice softer than he intended. "I wanted to make something more elaborate to surprise you, but this is all I came up with."

Chris's cheek turned crimson as she glanced at him through her lashes before looking back at the mug. She whispered, "It's fabulous." He reached in, pulling out the shirt with the picture of her on it. "Oh, my goodness, these are wonderful! Look, I didn't even pose like this. That 3D machine of yours really takes my picture in 3D. You can pose me in any way you want? That's awesome." Dan scratched his head, delighted she found an explanation for herself. Chris's duplicate remembering to pack them impressed Dan, since he doubted he would have thought of it himself. Chris broke his daze once more, this time by placing a kiss on the cheek. "Thanks, this is so perfect. I couldn't have imagined a better," she paused, her blush deepening as she tucked a loose strand of her hair behind her ear, "date?"

He grinned. "You're welcome," he said as he reached into the basket and grabbed the

Sandwiches, handing one to her. He opened the champagne bottle and poured out some carbonated juice in her plastic "glass".

She took a bite, smiling at the sandwich. "These are just the way I would have done them."

A twinge of guilt zapped through his heart, but he could not help but smile, watching Chris finally be there next to him. But the guilt made sure not to stay away for long, reminding him of how he cheated his way to her heart.

Chris shook her head, beaming. "It's perfect. I can't believe how many times I'm saying the word 'perfect'! You keep surprising me today. This is as good as it can get."

"Refill?" he offered, hoping to take his mind off things. She reached out her cup for him to fill, then took a sip with both hands on the cup, looking at him admiringly as she drank. Dan could not remember seeing her so happy like this before. "There is something different about you. Wonderfully different. I haven't even heard you stutter once," she praised, making Dan smile. However, he wondered why he was not feeling more like what he felt when he was with the double. He knew he should be more content being there with Chris, the real one.

Cupping her hand in his for a moment, "Thank you. I've been thinking of this moment for a long time. I'm glad we finally got together."

"Me too," she said, reaching for another sandwich, scooting closer to him. She leaned her head on his shoulders.

They spent the afternoon talking, reminiscing, and playing games. He had missed with Christy because of being drenched, spending so much time in the water. The air was warm, the breeze soft, and the spot he'd chosen—so carefully, so deliberately—was everything he hoped it would be. Chris was easy to talk to. Her laughter came freely, her stories pulled him in like familiar songs. She even remembered little things about their letters, things he'd long forgotten until she brought them up with a smile.

But no matter how much he tried to stay grounded in the moment, Dan's mind kept drifting. Now and then, his gaze would fall on the stream beside them—the water gently rushing over smooth stones, the exact stream he'd avoided stepping into this time. Last time, it had pulled him in, and he'd laughed with someone who wasn't really here now. A part of him wondered—if he had stepped into the water today, would it have shocked him awake? Made him feel more real? More present?

He forced himself to focus. Chris—the real Christy—was here. This moment, this carefully planned day, it was what he'd wanted. And yet... something tugged at the back of his mind. A strange hollowness, like a slightly off-keynote, tugged at him. Everything was perfect—the setting, the timing, even the way she looked at him—but he couldn't shake the absence of something he couldn't name. Or maybe, deep down, he could.

As the sky deepened into soft oranges and pinks, painting the clouds in a dreamy glow, Chris leaned gently against him, her head on his shoulder. He felt her warmth, the comfort of her presence. "This has been perfect," she whispered, voice low and full of peace. Dan nodded slowly, forcing a smile. He wanted so badly to agree—to feel that same completeness—but instead, all he could think about was how something so beautiful could still feel just a little... incomplete.

Dan smiled, wrapping an arm around her. "Yeah," he said, though the word felt hollow in his throat.

Almost on cue, the sky darkened further, and the scent of rain thickened in the air. Chris laughed as the first few drops fell. "Looks like we've got to move fast!"

They scrambled to pack up as the drizzle turned into a steady rainfall. Chris pulled on her coat, still smiling, her laughter ringing out as they hurried back to the car, kids yelling and laughing in the background.

Chapter 15

Between Two Realities

ON THE DRIVE BACK, Chris enthusiastically recounted the picnic, breaking the silence with stories and warmth. Outside, the rain intensified, softly drumming against the windshield, while the wipers moved rhythmically as the only other noise between them. Dan listened, nodding and smiling at appropriate times, though his reactions seemed more automatic than genuine. Chris spoke about her dance and casually mentioned how she would much rather go with him, admittingly Mark might not be so right for her; especially, according to Tina. Dan simply smiled as she went on catching him up with minor events in her life. The road shimmered under the streetlights, slick with rain, and he tightened his grip on the wheel, his thoughts distant. The air inside the car was warm, but Dan felt an odd chill settle over him, a quiet dissonance he couldn't shake. As they pulled up in front of Chris's house, the wipers made one final sweep before shutting off. Dan's hands instinctively clenched around the steering wheel as his gaze locked onto another car parked in the driveway. His stomach sank. Chris's voice, which had been so light just moments ago, suddenly faltered. "Oh no," she muttered under her breath, her entire demeanor shifting. "Mark's here."

Dan's posture stiffened instantly. "Do you want me to come in?"

Chris quickly shook her head, squeezing his hand. "No, you should go before he comes out." She hesitated before adding, "Sometimes he's... unreasonable when he drinks." Dan's jaw tightened. He wanted to stay, to make sure she was okay, but Chris gave him a small, reassuring smile. "My folks are here. I'll be fine." He didn't move right away, reluctant to let her walk into that house alone. But then Chris leaned in, pressing a soft kiss to his forehead. "Thanks for today," she whispered, her voice filled with something deeper than gratitude. He watched as she stepped out of the car, walking toward the front door. She turned once, waving before slipping inside. Dan sat there for a few seconds longer, his hands still resting on the wheel. With a quiet sigh, he shifted the car into gear and drove away, the scent of rain lingering in the air. Everything had gone perfectly today. No surprises. No stumbles. So why did something still feel missing? The rain continued to fall, blurring the glow of streetlights against the slick pavement. His wipers beat a steady rhythm, but it did nothing to clear the fog in his mind. His heart felt heavy, weighed down by the quiet ache of something unfinished—something slipping through his fingers. The rain had soaked through his sleeves as he stepped out of the car. He hardly noticed, absorbed in his thoughts, yet the cold, wet sensation lingered on his skin as he headed indoors.

Christy sat on the couch, curled up with her arms around herself, her eyes puffy from tears. Dan felt a surge of joy at seeing her, yet his heart ached at the same time. He silently approached, took a seat next to her, and gently rested a hand on her back. "Hey, I'm back," he softly said. Christy looked up at him, her eyes glistening as she tried to smile. For a moment, she studied him—his damp hair, the way he absently rubbed at his sleeve. Without thinking, she reached over to the armrest, grabbing the small towel she'd left there earlier and pressing it lightly into his hands.

"Oh no, did you fall into the stream again?" she said, smiling, remembering their date. Dan just shook his head, smiling too. "So, how was your date?" she asked, her voice shaky.

Dan hesitated, then took a deep breath. "It was... well," he paused, "she said it was perfect," he said, his voice breaking. Christy nodded with a forced smile, her gaze dropping, as if the thought of him agreeing was too much to bear. "But. . . it wasn't as perfect as ours." Dan stood up. Christy stared at him, masking a smile, her eyes filled with confusion. Dan leaned closer, his gaze intense. "When I'm with you, I'm not worried about saying the wrong thing. I'm just me. And that's enough."

Christy's eyes brimmed with tears once more, her voice trembling as she whispered, "You're doing it again. Running away, trying to take the easy way out again!" The fear gnawed at her heart, the dread that he was choosing a mere reflection, a duplicate, while his genuine desire remained with the original. Her chest tightened with the thought that he might always yearn for what they once had.

Dan shook his head, his heart pounding with urgency. "No. Not this time." He pulled her closer, his hand gently lifting her face so their eyes locked. "It was like going out with your twin and not you! She likes me. I saw it in her eyes, so I'm not taking the easy way out. I feel like, It would be easier to go back to her," Dan admitted. "If I end up with her, I could make it work, but I would miss you all the time!" His voice grew more intense, "Staying with you... though that might be harder with all the hiding questions, so much uncertainty. But I want to face all of that—with you, even if it gets a little messy sometimes." Filled with earnest emotion. "I love you, Christy. All of you! Everything about you!"

As he spoke, Christy's tears spilled over, now happy tears tracing paths down her cheeks. Her heart longed for that reassurance, for a love that chose her above all else. Christy's eyes widened with a mixture of surprise and overwhelming emotion, her heart pounding like a drum in her chest as she wrapped her arms tightly around his neck. "I'm so in love with you, too," she professed wholeheartedly, her voice brimming with sincerity and warmth. The words tumbled out, raw and earnest, as she drew a deep, steadying breath. "I know what we should do, the responsible thing, to just have me de-duplicated," she continued, her voice faltering slightly with the gravity of the decision. "But I... I want to live this through, with you!" Her confession hung in the air, ripe with vulnerability and hope. She paused for a moment, her eyes searching his, filled with both fear and excitement. "So, what do we do from here?"

Chapter 16

The Dance and Near Misses

DAN WALKED TO THE mailbox while Christy was preparing breakfast. The morning air was warm but comfortable, and Dan couldn't help but feel a sense of peace as the sun beamed down on him. He grabbed the mail, flipping through the usual flyers and junk mail. As he walked back inside, he enjoyed the cool breeze of his home, feeling thankful for the things taken for granted. He set the mail on the table.

"Oh! These are the shoes I wanted to buy for the dance. They're on sale now!" Christy exclaimed, glancing at an ad she saw while setting the breakfast table.

Dan looked at the picture she held up, smirking. "Wow. That is a good deal. I can afford that," he said, teasing her. Christy laughed, rolling her eyes. "What size are you?" Dan asked.

"I'm a size six and a half. Wow! I can't believe the dance is tonight!" she said, her voice filled with excitement. She sat next to Dan with her plate of breakfast. "And I still can't believe that I'm not de-duplicated." She gave him a playful look, her eyes twinkling with flirtation.

Dan tried to keep a straight face, but the corners of his mouth turned up, and soon both of them broke out laughing. It felt good to share such a moment—one where they couldn't forget, even if just for a moment, the complexity of their situation.

"What's this?" Christy asked, picking up a small white box with a red bow that Dan had set on the table when she wasn't looking. Dan gestured for her to open it. Christy's lips formed an 'o' as she untied the bow, her face brightening as she lifted the lid. Inside was a delicate silver necklace with a small heart pendant. Her smile was radiant as she gently pulled it out. "It's beautiful," she whispered, her eyes shining.

Dan smiled, a warmth spreading through his chest. "It's from Mr. Pemberton," he explained. "He added a special chip to it that gives you access to the car and the entire house, including the lab." He paused, looking at her. "Also, he said to give it to my true love." Christy hesitated, her fingers brushing over the pendant. Christy looked up at Dan, her eyes filled with emotion. He continued, "I don't think I've ever felt this happy." Dan slipped the necklace around her neck." her smile widening. Dan reached over, taking her hand in his. "I would love to spend the rest of my life with you," he said, his voice steady but filled with hope. He watched her carefully, his heart pounding. "I hope you feel the same way about me."

Christy looked down, her cheeks flushed as she nodded. "I do," she finally said, lifting her eyes to meet his. Her gaze softened as she added with a smirk, "Otherwise, I might be de-duplicated." Her grin turned mischievous, and Dan couldn't help but laugh, his heart feeling lighter.

But then her smile faltered, replaced by a look of sadness. "You know," she began, her voice quieter, "knowing I won't be able to see my family again is hard. It's comforting to know they won't miss me, but... I wish I could say goodbye. One last time, just for closure." Her face twitched as she tried to fight back tears.

Dan squeezed her hand gently. "I know," he said, his voice full of empathy. He paused, then said, "You know, the dance is tonight, right?" Christy nodded. Dan smiled. "I have an idea, but it means getting you a dress." He grinned. "If we can find the dress you were supposed to wear, I think we can pull this off."

Christy's eyes widened with excitement, already understanding his plan. "Okay, let's try it," she said, her voice eager.

After breakfast, they drove to the new K-Mart, a few miles not too far from town. "That's where I bought the dress." She said as they drove. "They also had the cutest shoes, but they were too expensive." She sighed wistfully. "They're on sale now, though! But I guess I won't be needing them anymore. "

Dan glanced at her, "It's so close to your. . .Chris's house," he pointed out. "I'm not sure if we should risk it." Dan pointed out.

"Remember, we checked everywhere. That was the only place that had it," she said, shrugging. "Besides, why would I be there?" referring to Chris, "She already has the dress. Besides, it's early. She's probably still sleeping." She reassured.

"You're not sleeping." He playfully pointed out.

"Well, it depends on the circumstance." She defended.

Dan sighed, but eventually nodded. "Fine. But let's make it quick, okay? In and out. I don't want to take any chances."

They parked and hurried into the store, their hands clasped together. "Wow, it's so empty. We're practically the first ones here," Christy noted, her voice full of excitement. "It feels like the entire store is ours! Come on, the dress is this way." She dragged Dan behind her, his fingers just managing to grab a cart before she sped off.

"Slow down," he said, trying to keep up.

"In and out, remember?" Christy said, her voice teasing.

They reached the aisle with the dresses, and Christy grabbed the one she wanted, holding it up against herself. "What do you think?" she asked, striking a few poses. Dan smirked, raising his brows and nodding his head with approval.

"You look amazing," he sincerely said. "You're going to be the prettiest one there." Referring to Chris. Christy smiles and nods.

"Well, now that I'll be staying with you, I'm going to need more clothes." The look of contentment on her face flooded Dan with glee, realizing her true love for him.

"I should take you shopping more often," he joked, and they both laughed as they moved through the store. They strolled down the aisles, Christy occasionally adding items to the cart. When they reached the underwear section, she nudged Dan's arm. He looked up, meeting her mischievous gaze. Then, before he knew it, she was thrusting a pair of underwear in his face. "How about these?" she asked, her eyes sparkling with mischief.

Dan's face turned bright red. "Uh... I'll be in the sports department," he stammered, backing away to give her a bit of privacy. Christy's laughter echoed through the store, warming Dan's heart.

Dan had decided to surprise Christy by buying the shoes she wanted while she was busy. "All these look the same," he thought as he tried to remember the K-mart as she had shown him. "Here it is. That is a good sales price... Now what size?...ahh, I think...six and a half" He thought to himself, only finding one pair of size five, one pair of size six and two pairs of size seven, grabbing a box of size seven leaning downwards to see if some were misplaced on the shelf.

"Hey you... what are you doing here?" He heard Christy say from behind.

"Oh, Christy! Just looking for some shoes... I didn't expect to see you here. You finished shopping?" casually placing the box behind his back. He tried pretending that he was looking for himself but at the wrong section, so as to not ruin her surprise. Dan finally looking at her, his eyes glanced over her clothes. They were different, somewhat worn, and not what she had walked in with. His face froze. Panic set in when he noticed she wasn't wearing the necklace he had given her.

"Chris!" His voice cracked, "Ahh, Christy, how are you!? What are you doing here!?"

"Just came to buy some shoes. They're on sale now, more affordable." She smiled curiously. "I had such a great time at our picnic. I didn't hear from you so I'm going with Mark." she blushed, turning toward the shoe rack, "I'm a size six and a half but I like to buy a size seven cause they fit more comfortably. Oh, look, only one more left." then looking up at him. "Are you ok?" Her concern lifted, noticing the size seven shoes he was holding behind him. Her smile is curious now, "you—couldn't have been getting those, for me?, — Did Tina tell you?" her smile widening.

"Yeah, yeah... I'm mean — No!" Dan reacted more nervously than normal. "I must be in the wrong section," he said, pretending to be looking for the Men's section. "Are you here by yourself?"

"No, my mom's with me, she's in the lingerie aisle. . . Are you sure you're ok?" she was concerned, grabbing his arm as if he were going to fall. "You look flush?" Dan just stood there panic-stricken.

"Oh! no, I'll be fine. You're just so radiant, even so early in the morning." She blushed, smiled and turned to face away. "I'd better go. I'll see you later!" Dan hid the shoes on a towel rack display shelf.

Christy reached for some underwear and turned toward her cart. Looking up as she nearly bumped into someone. "Mom!?" Christy exclaimed with her eyes wide open.

"I'm sorry honey, I didn't mean to frighten you." Linda said, reaching out to comfort her.

"No...No! I just didn't expect you there!"

"Did you find the shoes you were looking for?"

"Shoes?...Oh shoes...No" realizing the shoes are now on sale. Christy put her arms around her mother's neck with a hug of relief, realizing that her mom suspected nothing and the happiness of seeing her again.

"Wow, I must have really startled you," Linda smiled, "are you okay, honey?"

"Yes, I'm fine. Just wanted to look at this underwear?" She said, showing the undergarment.

"Oh, honey, you don't need any of those. You have plenty at home. You just bought some a few weeks ago." Noticing the cart with the dress, "is this your cart?"

"Umm...I thought I'd try it on to see how the shoes would look with it!" Christy thought fast

"That's a good idea. That's a nice outfit," her mom said, stepping back and looking at her clothes. Christy eyes opened wide then smiled, "Oh yeah this, I wasn't going to buy it, I just wanted to try it on, I'll go change, bye mom!" She said as she leaned to kiss her mom on the cheek and headed towards the changing room. Her mom just smiled, shook her head, and continued shopping.

Dan went to warn Christy at the lingerie aisle and nearly bumped into her mom. "Dan, how nice to see you! How are you?" She asked.

"Fine, how are you!?" his eyes were wide opened

"I must be doing really well. Everyone seems to be drawn to me today." She laughed at her own joke. "You just missed Christy. She went into the dressing room. You should wait. I'm sure she'd like to see you."

"Oh, I already ran into her a little while ago." Dan replied, Linda looked confused, "but I really must be going" he said looking toward the dressing room, "got to go, nice seeing you sorry I can't stay, bye" he rushed toward the Dressing room then heard a 'Pst!' coming from the other side of the makeup rack. Relieved to see Christy there, he looked back to see her mom shopping, and he hurried to the other side of the rack. "I just ran into you and your mom!"

"I know, I just ran into my mom!" Christy said, trying to suppress a smile. She was so happy to see her mom. After reading Dan's concern on his face she said, "Don't worry, she thought I was...well, me!." She smiles her cute smile, "Shh quiet, here I come!" she said looking though one of the rack holes pointing as Chris approached her mom. Come on, let's get out of here." Christie's whispered sneak away towards the exit.

"I just saw Dan. He was in quite a hurry," he heard Linda say to Chris.

"Yeah, so did I, but he was acting weird. . . well weirder than normal." He heard Chris say them both, laughing at the remark.

"You found your shoes?" Linda asked

"Yeah, they're so pretty, look. . . I think Dan was going to surprise me with the shoes, but who can tell with him." Dan could hear Chris say faintly as he quietly rushed towards Christy. Christy looked at Dan from the corner of her eye, smiling as they exited the store. They both started laughing. Dan grabbed Christie's hand and ran to the car. He opened the car doors remotely with his keys tag.

"That was too close!" Christy laughed as they put on their seat belts. "So, what do we do now?" They sat there in their car for a moment. Then Dan drove off, away from the store's parking lot. "Look, they're leaving. Should we go back?" They both stared at one another as if analyzing the possibilities. Then, smiling and with one quick nod, they headed back to the store. "Oh, and since the shoes are on sale, we should buy it!" Christy added. They hurried to the abandoned cart, then headed to the shoe aisle.

"You grab the clothes, and I'll bring the car around," Dan instructed, handing her money for her purchase. He knew the shoe size she wanted was out of stock. To buy the shoes he had hidden in the towel rack display, Dan discreetly dashed off. The timing worked out perfectly, having enough time to pay for the shoes and discreetly hide them in the car's trunk, then brought the car around closer.

The cashier at K-mart kept glancing at Christy, recognizing her from before. Christy avoided eye contact, hoping the cashier wouldn't mention anything. She quickly made her way to the car.

"They only had a size five left over," she complained to Dan. Then she smiled excitedly. "We did it. I got the dress and some extra clothes. This was fun! I wonder if we're going to have adventures like this all the time?" They both glanced at each other, eyes wide in wonder. They laughed as they put on their seat belts, talking about the adventure all the way home.

Pulling up to the driveway "Well, I'll just grab these," she said as she grabbed three large bags from the back seat. Dan smiled and gestured to her not to wait. He went around to the trunk and grabbed his jacket, concealing her surprise shoes.

Christy was putting the clothes away in her room when Dan walked in. He discreetly placed the shoes under the dress she had laid out on the bed when she wasn't looking. She smiled, finally noticing him, and continued to enjoy organizing her clothes in the closet. He watched for a while as she removed the tags from the clothes before placing them in their corresponding piles. He let her know he was going down to the basement to tend to the rabbit. A short while later, he fixed some small sandwiches similar to what they had at the picnic and placed them in a small pile on a dish. He took a couple and sat down on the couch thinking about how fortunate he felt, reminiscing while enjoying his sandwich.

"Oh, nice!" Christy exclaimed, grabbing the plate of sandwiches and then sitting next to Dan. They talked a little and laughed about their adventure, then silence satisfied in just having each other's company. "I'm excited about tonight, but I'm a little nervous, too. Why am I nervous?" Dan sat there on the couch, listening. He thought it could be because this could be the last goodbye, the last time she'll see her family. He sat there sad for her but only gave a half smile, shrugging his shoulders. "You know, I've been thinking, why was I, you know Chris, at K-mart today? She has everything for the dance. I bet she saw the shoe sale ad and went to buy those shoes." She said, grabbing another sandwich Dan had set beside the bed. "Do you think we should go back to see if they'd re-stocked those shoes?" Then convincing herself after a brief pause, "They'll probably won't even notice the shoes," referring to her family, "I'll be in and out so fast."

Chapter 17

Holding On by Letting Go

IT WAS GETTING CLOSE to the dance, Christy's chance to say goodbye to her family. Christy reached for the dress, her fingers brushing against the soft fabric, and lifted it towards her with a delighted smile. "Oh my god, the shoes!" Her voice was full of excitement, echoing the brightness of her eyes. Dan watched as her face lit up, the sheer joy radiating off of her. It was almost as if the shoes themselves, simple and elegant, grew even more beautiful just by being near her.

She picked up one shoe, with no paper wadding, and peered inside at the small tag. "And you got them in the right size! How'd you know?" she asked, her eyes finding his, a mix of surprise and gratitude.

Dan gave her a knowing smile, a hint of pride dancing in his gaze. "You know, it's ironic how the original girl was the one who taught me something for the double," he said, his voice softened by nostalgia.

Christy laughed, her attention briefly shifting back to the shoes. She grabbed the other shoe, gently removing the paper wad inside. "I love them, thank you. They're perfect," she said, her voice softening at the last word.

But as she held the wad of paper, something shifted. It felt heavier than it should. She slowly opened the rapper, looking at Dan, who just sat there with a half-nervous grin on his face that she found so adorable. Slowly, she unwrapped the paper. A gasp escaped her lips, and her eyes widened as she realized what she was holding.

"Oh my god," she whispered, her eyes filling with tears. Her heart pounded, and her smile stretched wide as she looked at Dan, then back to the ring box, anticipation building with every breath. She opened it, and the tears spilled over as she saw the ring—the ring, the one she had dreamed of, the one she had written to him about all those months ago. She turned to him, her entire being overwhelmed with love and joy. Barely able to contain herself, she gave an excited jump.

"Oh my god," she repeated, her voice shaking. Her eyes met his, and she nodded, her tears and smile already conveying her response. Dan got up from the bed and moved toward her, and she flung herself into his embrace. They held each other tightly, his hands securing her as he softly expressed his love. He recounted the instant he first realized his love for her, how his feelings deepened with each letter and every small moment they shared. He told her she was the one person. Through all their recent adventures and experiences together, even as a clone, competing against her original self, Christy prevailed in winning Dan's heart, understanding him better than anyone else.

His voice dropped, his tone serious. "I know you'll never be able to see your parents or your family again after tonight. In one of your letters, you said you'd want to be proposed to while on their knees, in your home, surrounded by everyone who loves you," Dan said, dropping to one knee before her. "I know my love for you is greater than my love for anyone else. And if your love for me is just as deep, then everyone in this room—just us—is all that matters." He held up the ring. "Christy, I want to spend the rest of my life with you. Not with Chris or anyone else. Just you. I love you. Will you marry me?"

Christy's tears ran freely now, her lips trembling as she looked at the ring. "This is so perfect," she managed to say, her voice breaking. She took a deep breath, trying to steady herself. "I couldn't have wished for a better proposal. Even though my family isn't here to see this—this... the way everything is right now—it's perfect." She nodded, her tears spilling as she smiled. "Yes, I'll marry you."

Dan, still down on one knee, slipped the ring on her finger. He got up, and they both leaned in, their lips meeting in a tender, love-filled kiss, sealing the promise between them. The Grandfather clock struck half pass, and they both knew they had to hurry.

She laid the dress over the bed. She set the shoes on the floor just below the dress. And Dan shut the door behind him. Christy changes rather quickly, to Dan's surprise. "You look beautiful." Dan said. She gave a little catwalk turn, pretending to be modeling the outfit. She walked up to him and gave him a soft kiss on the lip. "Wow," he said softly, "what was that for?" She looked down at her shoes.

The car ride to her parents' house was silent, filled with a mild tension neither of them spoke of. The plan was simple—wait for Chris and Mark to leave for the dance, then run in to say goodbye to her family. They parked in the vacant lot behind the house, directly across from her parents' home, having a direct view of her parents' house across the street.

"You think they already left?" Dan whispered, his voice barely audible.

Christy laughed. "I don't think you have to whisper. I'm pretty sure they can't hear you from here." Dan blushed, and she reached over to give his arm a gentle squeeze. "You're so cute," she said, smiling. "But I doubt they've left yet. Mark's never early."

As if on cue, Mark's car turned the corner, his attention visibly distracted by a couple of girls walking down the dirt road. "He's such a creep. I don't know what she sees in him," Christy muttered, her voice laced with frustration.

Dan raised an eyebrow at her, knowing full well that Chris was technically her double. Christy leaned back, crossing her arms defensively. "Well, I don't," she added, and they both shared a smile.

Mark pulled up to the house and started honking his horn frantically. "Come on, let's go!" he shouted, his face poking out the window, dark shades covering his eyes. Christy and Dan exchanged a glance, both shaking their heads in disapproval. Chris burst out the door, barely managing to put her shoes on as she ran. They could hear her yell, "Bye!" to her parents.

"Hurry up!" Mark yelled again, his impatience palpable. The disgust on Christy and Dan's faces was obvious. Then Tina ran out of the house, lipstick in hand. Dan and Christy exchanged a look—they hadn't expected Tina to be there. Dan watched the scene, recalculating their plan. Christy just looked at him, her own tension easing as his face softened, the worry disappearing.

Dan nodded, indicating they could continue as planned. Chris held the door for Tina, who barely got in before Mark peeled away, tires spinning and dust flying in a massive cloud.

They watched as Chris's mom peeked out through the screen door. "We don't have to do this, you know," Christy said softly, her gaze on her mother. "She saw them leave."

"No, we just have to be quick," Dan replied. "And make sure no one comes outside." Christy nodded, looking down at her engagement ring. She slipped it off, giving Dan a look that said, "That was close." Dan raised his brows, as if to say, 'Good catch'.

She opened the car door, pausing for just a breath. "Oh, and the necklace," Dan said, holding out his hand gently. "And... try not to cry, okay?" His voice was soft, barely holding steady.

CHRISTY LOOKED AT HIM, her eyes already glistening, and managed a small nod. She slipped the necklace into his palm, then smiled—a fragile, trembling smile.

Inside the house, everything was exactly as she remembered. Her dad was in the living room, his feet up, half-watching the TV. Little Kathy sat on the floor, surrounded by a rainbow of toys, humming to herself in a world of make-believe. Her mom moved around in the kitchen, the sound of running water and clinking dishes grounding the air.

The front door creaked as Christy pushed it open.

Her dad looked up first. "Hey, pumpkin. I thought you left already."

She stood there for a moment, the lump in her throat growing unbearable. "I... I forgot something," she said. But her voice cracked, and it betrayed her. "I forgot to say goodbye."

Her dad furrowed his brow. "Didn't you already—?"

She cut him off, rushing forward, arms wrapping tightly around him. "It was too fast. I didn't say it right," she whispered into his shoulder. "I love you so much, Dad."

Her mom came out of the kitchen, drying her hands. "Christy?" she asked, surprised by the sudden emotion.

Christy turned and threw her arms around her. "You too, Mom. I love you so much. I needed to say it properly."

Her mom froze for a second, then hugged her tightly, as if sensing something deeper was going on. "We love you too, honey," she said softly. "What's all this?"

Christy couldn't answer. The tears were falling freely now.

She knelt down beside her little sister. "Hey, Kathy," she said with a smile that barely held. "Come here, sweetheart."

Kathy climbed into her arms, giggling, unaware of the weight pressing on her sister's heart. Christy hugged her fiercely, breathing in the scent of crayons and baby shampoo. "I love you so much," she whispered, planting a kiss on her cheek. "Don't forget me, okay?"

She set her down gently, and with one last look at her family—burning it into memory and a quick smile—she turned and dashed out the door, pulling it shut behind her before she could change her mind.

Dan was still waiting, the car door open like a lifeline. She climbed in quickly, face streaked with tears. He said nothing—he just pulled away, taking a side street to avoid passing the front windows. Just in case her mom was watching.

The car was quiet. Christy stared out the window, her shoulders trembling as she tried to calm her breath. After a long pause, she looked over at Dan and gave him a soft, tear-stained smile.

"You okay?" Dan asked, his voice barely above a whisper as he held out both pieces of jewelry.

She nodded, tears still in her eyes. "I'm grateful I got to say goodbye," she said, her voice still emotional but more composed. "Thank you for being by my side and helping me overcome obstacles to bring me joy. You are my dream." She slipped the ring back onto her finger, holding it there for a moment as if to find stability in its weight. "I feel... relieved. Like a burden I was unaware of lifted itself."

She turned the necklace over in her hands. "Even though I'll never see them again," she added, "somehow it helps to know they'll still see me. That in their world, I'm still there, just... living life."

She looked up, eyes distant, a faint smile tugging at her lips. "It's weird. All of this is weird. But for the first time, I don't feel like I'm running. I feel like I left something right."

It was well past evening, and their stomachs rumbled, a reminder of the light lunch they had amidst all the shopping and excitement. They stopped at an upscale two-story restaurant on the outskirts of town, knowing it was unlikely they'd run into anyone she knew there. They danced formally, and she wore an appropriate outfit. Dan purchased a nice dress jacket, and they occasionally dance to their favorite songs. "You know," Christy whispered, her lips close to his ear, "this is exactly how I always imagined it would be. It's like I'm living in a dream." Dan agreed.

They danced for hours, losing track of time as they moved together, the rest of the world fading away. It was just them—two people who had found something special, something that felt truly real.

"This is nice," Christy said, looking out at the view. The window overlooked the town, the lights twinkling peacefully below. The scene was tranquil, a contrast to the emotions that had just swirled through her. Dan, meanwhile, couldn't take his eyes off her. Her lips looked full, and her hair caught the light just right. She was perfect, he thought. She caught him staring and blushed, her eyes turning away, her lips curling into a shy smile.

Dan felt his heart swell, overwhelmed by how lucky he was. They both felt like the only two people in the world, there together, sharing this moment of calm after the storm.

When they finally got back to the house, it was late, and the night air had a coolness that hurried them inside. The place was dark and quiet, a stark contrast to the lively evening they had just shared. Dan walked Christy to her bedroom door, treating it like the entrance to her own apartment. It felt sweet and mischievous, like two teenagers sneaking home after curfew. He paused at the threshold, their eyes locking in the dim light of the hallway. Leaning in, he gave her a goodnight kiss. It was tender, a gentle promise that lingered on her lips and sent butterflies fluttering wildly through Christy's stomach.

Christy smiled, happiness radiating from her eyes. "Goodnight, Dan." Her voice was a whisper, full of warmth. She watched him retreat down the hallway, each step echoing through the silent house. The further he went, the more she felt a sudden chill filling the space where he had been. She wanted to call him back, to hold him and never let him go, but she knew how much they both needed rest after such an emotionally charged day.

Slipping into her room, Christy felt as light as air, like a giddy schoolgirl with a secret too good to keep. She couldn't contain herself and jumped onto the bed, sitting on her knees with a wide grin that stretched across her face. She extended her hand in front of her, marveling yet again at the simple ring on her finger. It caught the light even in the dim room, a brilliant reminder of the promise she had made.

Her thoughts danced eagerly to the future, and her heart swelled at the prospect of the life she would have with Dan. It felt so good, so right—better than she had ever dared to imagine. She looked at the ring once more, biting her bottom lip as joy bubbled inside her. This—the love, the commitment, the sheer possibility of it all—was what she had been searching for, consciously or not, and now it was hers.

As she soaked in the euphoria, her thoughts wandered back to her family and to her best friend, Tina. A twinge of sadness tugged at her heart, like a small dark cloud against a bright sky. But she took comfort in knowing this was where she was meant to be. In a life crafted from both happiness and sacrifice. The knowledge that they'd never truly know her loss but would continue to see her double brought her a bittersweet sense of peace.

Worn out but overjoyed, she finally slipped under the covers. The fabric was cool against her skin, and she let out a long, contented sigh. As her eyes traced imaginary circles on the ceiling, her eyes felt heavy now, even though she found her mind too busy with the possibilities awaiting her. She yawned, stretching out her arms. Maybe she'd get some sleep after all.

Chapter 18

Unification

DAN, TOO, FELT RESTLESS. He couldn't sleep—his mind was buzzing with thoughts of Christy, of their dance, of their love. Downstairs, he found solace in the quiet of his lab. He checked on the rabbit, giving it fresh water and refilling its food. As he looked around, he remembered the day he had first stepped into this lab, how different everything had been back then.

He smiled to himself, feeling a sense of contentment. He thought he might de-duplicate the original rabbit, but somehow that felt wrong. Slowly, he began to disassemble the machine that had brought him to this point. It had served its purpose, and now it was time to move forward. He removed a few crucial parts, destroying them to ensure no one could ever use it again. Before heading up to bed, he took the rabbit up the elevator, setting it free in the backyard, placing a small bowl of water out in case it returned.

The morning arrived, serene and peaceful. Christy awoke to the soft blue light of dawn filtering through the curtains. She stretched, yawning, as the events of the previous night played in her mind, bringing a smile to her lips.

In the kitchen, Dan was already busy preparing breakfast—bacon, eggs, hash browns, and fresh orange juice. As Christy entered the kitchen, Dan looked over his shoulder, his gaze catching hers.

"Good morning," he said, his eyes lighting up at the sight of her. "Wow, you look beautiful."

Christy blushed, brushing her hair back. "Good morning," she replied, her voice soft. "Breakfast smells amazing."

Dan leaned in, placing a kiss on her cheek. "If this is how mornings are going to be, I should have proposed to you sooner," he said with a grin.

Christy laughed, giving him a playful look. "You're right about that." She sat down, glancing at the spread before her. "This is nice, Dan. Thank you." They ate together, their conversation flowing effortlessly, their laughter filling the room. Time seemed to pass by in the blink of an eye, and for the first time in a long time, everything felt right. After breakfast, they found themselves sitting on the couch, enjoying the calm of the morning. Dan looked over at Christy, his heart swelling with love. He reached for her hand, lacing his fingers with hers.

Christy looked at him, her eyes filled with tears. "I love you, Dan. I don't need anything else but you. Let's get married today." She leaned in, her lips meeting his in a soft kiss, one filled with all the love she felt. They planned out their day and, in that moment, they knew they had found something rare, something worth holding onto. And as they sat there, wrapped in each other's arms, they knew that whatever the future held, they would face it together. They sat for a moment, then Dan went downstairs to the basement to continue dismantling the machine.

The phone rang. Christy recognized the caller id and let the answering machine pick up. It was Chris calling, but she didn't leave a message. Shortly after, the phone rang again, recognizing the number she saw it was Tina calling. Her reaction was to answer the phone but stopped herself mid reach and let the answering machine answer. "Hello?...Hello!?. . . Dan!? Are you there? Pickup, you idiot, this is important!" Christy smiled at Tina's typical candor, "Dan!? Call me back as soon as you get this!" Tina sounded very upset. Christy couldn't help but feel sad knowing she couldn't do anything to help her friend in need. Christy erased the message.

The drive to Vegas flew by in a whirlwind of excitement. Anticipation, a shared sense of freedom and possibility crackling between them, captivated them both. Christy's face glowed with joy, a genuine, almost childlike wonderment in her eyes. "I'm so excited. It's like a dream come true, you know?" she exclaimed, her voice tinged with the giddy disbelief that comes with long-awaited moments finally coming to life.

The ceremony itself was brief—almost blink-and-you-miss-it fast—but, in its simplicity, deeply satisfying. It felt private, like a sacred vow shared only between their hearts, with no interruptions from the outside world.

Dan reached for her hands, his eyes soft with both relief and concern. "I hope this was okay. I know you would've preferred a bigger wedding with your family and friends around you."

Christy's radiant smile dimmed for just a heartbeat, and she looked down, a shadow of wistfulness crossing her face. "This was perfect, really. And besides, there are no distractions. It's just you and me." She hesitated, her gaze distant. "Though... I won't lie. It would've been nice to have my family and Tina here. To let them see how happy I am. I hate that they're caught up with Chris and Mark's issue back home. But...right here, right now? I've never been happier, Dan. I love you so much."

His heart ached with conflicting emotions. "I feel selfish," he admitted, squeezing her hands as if he could anchor himself to her warmth. "I took you from your entire life just to have you here with me. Sometimes I think, maybe if I. . . de-duplicated you and ran away with Chris. At least it would be like you could stay with your family. . ."

She laughed softly, shaking her head, and cut in, "She'd be with her family, Dan. But me? I wouldn't exist. That past version of myself feels like a stranger to me now. I'm here because I chose this life with you. You're my family now. Sure, I'll miss them, but knowing Chris is there brings me peace. It's like...my missing them is only half as heavy." She paused, searching for the right words, her voice gentle.

"They're not missing me. And somehow, that makes it easier." Then she added playfully, "I just feel bad for stealing Chris's true love, knowing she'll never be as happy as I am."

Dan admired her strength, her ability to embrace what seemed to him like an impossible decision. He saw in her a remarkable resilience, a positivity and acceptance that seemed to have a life of its own. Christy was more than just his partner; she was a force of nature, and the way she navigated this unique reality only deepened his love for her.

"Well, since Chris will not be as happy without me, what if we get rid of her somehow, and you can take her place?" Dan suggested with a grin.

"What's wrong with you!?" She playfully slapped his arm, and they both laughed at his impulsive, rashness idea.

Dan and Christy arrived at the hotel, a secluded, beautiful place nestled against a backdrop of soft, rolling hills. The lobby's warm lights gleamed, and a gentle, inviting lavender scent permeated the air. After the check-in, they walked hand in hand down the corridor to their suite, a cozy room with large windows that framed the night sky perfectly, casting a soft glow across the room.

Christy was the first to break the silence, her laughter lighting up the room as she teased, "Look at us—married, in a gorgeous room. This almost doesn't feel real." Her eyes sparkled as she leaned into Dan, who wrapped his arms around her, unable to help but smile at her happiness.

They explored the room together, laughing over the little details they found funny or charming. Dan opened the balcony door to let in the night air, which was cool and crisp, and Christy joined him, the two of them standing close as they gazed at the stars. The quiet felt like a cocoon, a moment just for them.

Eventually, they both relaxed on the couch, talking about everything and nothing. The conversation shifted to memories of when they first met, the brief moments that had brought them to this point. Their laughter softened, and Christy's hand found its way into Dan's fingers intertwined. The world outside seemed to fade, leaving only the two of them in their shared warmth.

Dan leaned forward, pressing a gentle kiss to her forehead. It was a small, tender gesture that felt somehow different, more meaningful. As the night continued, their touches grew more lingering, each kiss a little longer than the last. They took their time, cherishing the quiet joy of simply being together—every glance, every smile held its own gentle weight.

Eventually, the two moved to the bed, lying next to each other while continuing their soft-passionate kisses. As their eyes locked, Dan experienced a warm rush of gentle assurance. The moment felt perfect because of its serene magic, trust, and intimacy. Their first time together happened effortlessly and tenderly, each moment wrapped in the comfort of knowing they were exactly where they wished to be—together, creating a memory just for them.

Their breaths slowly returned to normal as they lay entwined in each other's arms, savoring the afterglow of their passionate joining. The world outside had no hold on them at this moment; it was just the two of them–together, creating a memory just for them.

Chapter 19

Caught in the Crossfire

THE NEXT MORNING, THE soft glow of the early sun peeked through the curtains, casting a gentle light over the room. Dan woke up to the sight of Christy beside him, her face peaceful and framed by loose strands of hair. He smiled, feeling a sense of quiet happiness, and gently brushed a hand across her cheek. Christy stirred, her eyes slowly fluttering open, and she smiled sleepily at him, pulling herself closer as they shared a warm, unspoken connection.

Their movements were gentle and unhurried, guided by an ease and familiarity that made everything feel natural. In the morning's quiet, they embraced, exploring their deepening bond, laughing softly as they exchanged quiet words. Their love felt deeper, more certain, as if each moment they spent together added another layer to their shared happiness.

They lay side by side, smiling at the ceiling, wrapped in the morning's warmth sun and their shared affection. When their stomachs eventually reminded them of breakfast, they ordered room service, enjoying the luxury of fresh fruit, warm pastries, and coffee brought to their door. They laughed as they ate, feeding each other bites of food and savoring the simplicity of being in each other's company.

After breakfast, they took a quick shower. After getting ready for the day, they explored the hotel's nearby shopping area.

They wandered through quaint shops, picking up small souvenirs that would forever remind them of this first trip together. Christy found a delicate bracelet, and Dan couldn't resist buying it for her, delighted by the way her eyes lit up. She surprised him by picking up a small leather notebook, knowing he liked to jot down ideas and notes.

As the day wore on, they made their way back to the car, both of them a little reluctant to leave but excited to begin their life together at home. They filled their drive back with laughter, shared stories, and quiet moments of contentment, comforted by the knowledge that they were returning home together to share countless more mornings and memories.

That evening, as the phone rang through the quiet of the house, Dan instinctively moved to pick it up. But Christy gently touched his arm, her expression uncertain. "It's probably Chris," she said softly. "She's been trying to call all day."

They shared a look, both fully aware of the complexities woven into their lives. Instead of answering, they let the phone ring, the sound hanging in the air until the answering machine picked up. Chris's voice filled the room, her tone soft but with a hint of urgency. "Hey, Dan... Mark proposed, and I...I really need to talk to you."

Her words lingered, heavy with the unspoken. Christy looked at Dan, her expression shadowed with a mix of emotions. She understood why Chris wanted to talk—she'd seen it before. Chris wasn't calling just to share news; she was reaching out, likely hoping Dan would offer her the kind of comfort and honesty that had been a staple in their friendship. She wanted his insight, his advice. And perhaps, deep down, she was looking for a reason to reconsider Mark's proposal, to weigh her feelings against the steady connection she'd always had with Dan.

Christy sighed, almost to herself, then said, "She wants you to talk her out of it. She's reaching out because she trusts you, because part of her probably wishes you would give her a reason not to marry Mark. I bet she's thinking about the picnic, about the way you two always seem to just...click." She hesitated, her voice lowering. "And if you call her back, there's a chance she'll fall for you all over again, Dan. She doesn't know you're...with me now. And I...I can't lose you to her."

Dan listened carefully, understanding her fears. He knew Christy was strong and optimistic, but the idea of him rekindling something with Chris, even unintentionally, was a risk she wasn't willing to take. The life they were constructing was delicate, resting on a base they had crafted themselves, shaped by decisions, serendipity, and the faith that they could sustain their love without glancing back. Dan took her hand, his resolve clear. "You're right," he said. "I won't return the call." The decision felt final, but as the machine clicked off, he couldn't deny the slight ache that came with it. Chris had been an important part of his life, someone he'd shared a deep connection with. But in that moment, he understood that the life he wanted was with Christy—the woman who chose to be by his side, who embraced all the tangled pieces of his life without hesitation.

They sat together in the quiet that followed; the choice settling over them like a silent promise. Christy rested her head on his shoulder, and they stayed like that for a while, letting go of the past as they looked ahead to a future they could finally claim as their own.

That evening, the doorbell rang and Christy looked at the small LCD peeping monitor next to the door. "Oh, my God!" she whispered quietly to Dan, "It's Tina!" Christy gestured she was going to hide in the room.

Dan opened the door to find Tina standing there with her face flushed, mixed with frustration and anguish. She barely waited for the door to fully open before pushing the door open, letting herself in and unleashing her emotions. "Where were you, Dan? Didn't you get any of my messages?! You could have stopped this! I thought you actually cared about her—and look what you let happen." Her voice cracked, and a few tears slipped down her cheeks as she fell into his arms, grief spilling over into anger and sorrow. "You're no genius, Dan. You're just a coward." She pulled away, brushing her tears aside.

As Dan listened, Tina explained the details he had missed. Chris had left a message telling Mark she didn't want to marry him. But Mark, ever persistent, had shown up at Chris's family's home, and in front of everyone, he proposed. In a whirlwind, he whisked Chris off to Vegas, and just like that, they're off to get married. "I didn't even get to be here for my best friend's wedding," Tina continued, her voice a raw whisper. "She's going to come back in a few days, but I don't know if she'll ever be the same."

He swallowed hard. Part of him wondered if it was fate that drove Chris to Vegas and without Tina, the same way it had drawn him and Christy there. Maybe inevitably, the tangled mess of their lives would keep pulling them toward decisions they hadn't fully prepared for.

Tina, meanwhile, was on her own journey. She loved Chris deeply. Dan felt the weight of her next words. "I'll stay a little longer for her. But it's killing me to see her treated so poorly, Dan. Mark...he's not who he seemed to be. He's only getting crueler, and...I can't watch her get ridiculed all the time. Why didn't you step up or at least return her call to talk her out of it? Between the both of us, she might have listened. If it gets to be too much, I won't be able to take much more. I think I might just have to leave somewhere out of here." Tina looked him over. "I'm surprised she hasn't come looking for you. You were easy to find. Anyway, we might be too late," she realized, then turned to leave. "See you never, bonehead!" the door closed behind her.

Dan looked at the monitor and saw Tina race away. It gnawed at him that his and Christy's happiness had such a bitter edge, built on a foundation that left so many others in pain.

As Christy comforted him, she confessed that staying in Arizona felt too close to their past, where memories and people from their former lives constantly resurfaced. Together, they decided to move, somewhere they could truly start anew. Christy picked a place she and Tina had once dreamed about, somewhere far from the noise and chaotic reach of everyone back home. It was a slower-paced, quieter place—somewhere that might offer them a real chance at peace.

Dan could feel the weight of the situation as much as Christy. They'd shared beautiful, fleeting moments together, but each day carried the reminder of the sacrifices they'd both made, and the cost seemed to grow heavier. They would start over, in a place that wasn't haunted by past loves, broken dreams, and guilt.

They began discussing their next steps. Together, they looked over maps and real estate listings, talking through their options until they found a town that felt just right. It was quaint and full of character, with a close-knit community and winding roads bordered by tall trees. It was a fresh start.

With the decision made, they hired movers to handle most of the work, ensuring their new home would be ready when they arrived. Dan took extra precautions to transport his delicate lab equipment in a rented van, while Christy followed behind in his car, eagerly envisioning how they'd decorate and settle into their new life. They would leave the house they were leaving behind sealed up and in the past—there would be little reason to return.

On the morning of the move, Dan felt determined, while Christy brimmed with excitement. In the days that followed, they settled into their new house, finding a rhythm between unpacking, decorating, and getting acquainted with their surroundings. Halloween was right around the corner, and Christy was already dreaming of setting up their new place with spooky decorations to entertain the local trick-or-treaters. She expressed a bit of disappointment to Dan that they might run out of time for Halloween decorating in their new neighborhood. Sensing her wish, Dan wasn't about to let her down. Dan was intelligent and high on creativity; he transformed empty moving boxes into haunted decoration. He painted them to resemble old wooden panels and used tape to arrange them around the house, giving it the appearance of a creepy abandoned mansion. Then, he placed frozen Dry Ice Bricks in buckets of water behind the bushes to create an eerie mist that would greet their visitors.

On Halloween night, Christy didn't have time to buy a witch's makeup and outfit, so Dan had her wear the dress she wore the night of the dance since she looked so stunning. Christy dressed as a beautiful princess, although she was skeptical. "How is this going to scare the kids?" she asked, hands on her hips with a playful pout. Dan just grinned, saying, "I'm sure they'll be terrified."

A haunting illusion greeted the first trick-or-treaters. Dan had set up a projector in the upstairs window, casting Christy's image as an alluring princess, only for the image to morph into a witch with a cackling laugh. At the front door, another projection showed a hunched-over, which slowly transformed back into the princess, holding a basket of candy. When the door opened, there stood Christy, smiling sweetly, but the children would scream and run back, then laugh, as they reached for the treat at arm's length.

The night was a massive hit. Some kids cried, some laughed, and a few ran away only to inch back to see the display again. Christy's eyes sparkled with joy, and after the last trick-or-treater had left, she hugged Dan tightly. "You're a genius," she whispered, grinning from ear to ear. The evening was everything she had hoped for and more, her heart full as they looked out over the quiet street, their new neighborhood already feeling like home.

Chapter 20

Surprise Reunion

SEVERAL MONTHS HAD GONE by since their move into the new house, and they had become quite familiar with the town. Christy loved it there. While Christy was out grocery shopping, Dan was busy with some house repairs. As Christy finished shopping and pushed her cart towards her car to load the groceries, she heard a familiar someone calling her name. Turning around, her eyes widening in surprise to see . . . "Tina?!"

Tina stared at her, equally stunned. "Christy? How is this even possible?" She embraced Christy, but quickly stepped back, inspecting her. "You look different—your skin, your size. You weren't like this just a few weeks ago. Last I saw you."

Christy felt panic rising but fought to maintain an appearance of calm, knowing how unlikely she would be to fool Tina. She swallowed hard, forcing composure. "Oh, Tina," she replied, her voice strained as she crafted an explanation. "It's amazing what a little self-care can do, right?" She injected a nervous laugh at the end, desperately trying to turn the attention elsewhere. "You have to tell me what you've been up to," she pushed, hoping to shift focus. But Tina's eyes remained sharply fixed on her, suspicion growing more clear. A knowing look crossed Tina's face as she suddenly stepped backward. She glanced toward the parking lot and made a determined move toward a payphone. "No, Tina, wait!" Christy shouted, lunging towards Tina in a panic. Her heart pounded as she tried to reach her in time. The possibility of Tina making that call spread terror through her. "Please, don't call her. I can explain!" she yelled again, her voice edged with desperation. Her hands trembled as she grabbed the payphone, pulling it away.

Tina frowned, reluctant but momentarily swayed by the desperation in Christy's eyes. She let go of the phone, her expression tinged with both confusion and anger. Clearly, something was amiss, and she would not let it go until she got answers.

"Explain what, exactly?" Tina's demand was sharp. Her patience was wearing thin, and she crossed her arms, waiting for a reasonable answer. Christy knew she would need to act quickly to contain the situation and had to come up with a convincing story.

Her mind raced through plausible explanations, each one more implausible than the last. She could tell that Tina wouldn't believe her without knowing the full story. But how much was safe to reveal? Sweat beaded on her forehead as she weighed her options.

Christy glanced around cautiously before leaning in and whispering, "Not here. Let's pack up the car and head to my place. I promise to spill everything there." Tina hesitated but agreed, trailing behind Christy to the car. She then went to retrieve her own vehicle while Christy packed the groceries into her trunk. By the time they got back to the house, Christy's stomach was in knots. She parked the car and led Tina inside. The two friends placed the grocery bags up and sat on the couch, Tina waiting expectantly, her arms crossed. Christy took a deep breath and began explaining everything—about Dan's duplicator, about being a copy of the original Christy. How Dan was supposed to deduplicate her but instead fell in love. Tina's jaw dropped, her eyes flicking from Christy to the front door, as though expecting someone to burst in yelling, "Surprise!"

"You're serious!?" Tina finally managed to say.

"Yes." Christy's voice was soft, her eyes filled with both regret and hope. "I know it's a lot to take in, but this is real. I need you to understand."

Before Tina could respond, Dan walked into the living room, freezing when he saw Tina. His face went pale. "Uh... hey, Tina." He gave an awkward smile, clearly surprised.

Tina raised an eyebrow. "So, knucklehead, care to fill me in on why you played Dr. Frankenstein with my best friend?"

Dan looked at Christy, who gave him an apologetic smile. He sighed and sat down, running a hand through his hair. "It's . . . complicated, Tina."

"I bet it is," Tina said, her voice dripping with sarcasm.

Christy reached for Tina's hand. "We've stayed away from everyone to avoid complications," she explained. "But... I miss my family. I miss seeing them. And I missed you so very much, Tina. "

Tina gazed at her with softened eyes. "Christy, well, the other Christy turned to food as a way to handle Mark's abuse and has gained a lot of weight. She's falling apart, constantly depressed, and I can't recall the last time I saw her smile. As for your mom, Christy—Linda—she isn't doing well. And Mark's behavior has..." She paused, her voice breaking. "It's gotten worse. I've noticed him following me sometimes, especially when he's drunk, and he has made several unwanted advances toward me! He's disgusting."

"I'll say!" Dan interjected, then quickly corrected himself, aware it might seem like an insult to Tina. "I mean about Mark. I should have realized he'd still be causing trouble."

Tina looked at him, her eyes narrowing. "You created this problem, this whole mess, bonehead! The least you could do is fix it. They need to know that Christy is okay. Even if it's just... you." She nodded toward Christy.

Dan paused, looking over at Christy. Her eyes were brimming with tears, and her expression was one of yearning. He let out a sigh. "Alright," he eventually agreed. "We'll come up with a plan. But we need time, and we must be cautious—no one else can know." Tina nodded, a wave of relief spreading across her features. "Thank you," she said earnestly.

As the days passed, everything seemed to settle into place—until one quiet evening. Dan and Christy were curled up on the couch, the soft flicker of the television casting lazy shadows across the room. A sudden knock shattered the calm. Dan stood, confused, and opened the door. His blood ran cold. Tina stood there—her lip bruised, arms trembling. Beside her was Chris, the original, just as shaken. And behind  them, stepping forward with a slow, sinister grin, was Mark.

"Well, here we are," Mark said, forcing his way inside and revealing a pistol at his side. He waved it just enough to make his point. "Looks like we've got unfinished business. Everyone—sit down."

Christy entered the room from the hallway just in time to see Mark. Her face went pale, horror blooming as she saw Tina and Chris in distress. Dan instinctively moved closer to her, shielding her with a glance.

Dan's fists clenched. "How did you find us?"

Mark smirked. "Been following Tina for weeks."

Tina's eyes widened. "Me? Why the hell would you drive this far for me?!"

Mark turned his gaze to Christy. "It doesn't matter now."

He lunged forward and seized Christy's arm, pulling her toward him roughly.

"She's mine," he hissed, eyes locked on Dan with venom.

"LET GO OF HER!" Dan shouted, rushing forward.

Mark pointed the gun at Chris and fired, hitting her leg. The deafening bang echoed through the room. Mark yelled, "This pathetic excuse for a dame is all yours!" as Chris screamed in agony and collapsed to the floor. "I'm keeping the new one." He sneered.

"No!" Christy screamed. Mark twisted her arm behind her back, forcing her down. Dan's hands shook as he tried to think of a way to stop this nightmare.

Dan's eyes locking onto Christy. The desperation in her eyes tore at him. He couldn't let Mark take her. With a surge of adrenaline, Dan tackled Mark, knocking the gun from his hand. They struggled on the ground, each trying to get control of the weapon. Christy and Tina screamed, rushing to Chris, who was barely conscious, blood pooling around her leg.

In the chaos, another shot rang out. Dan froze, feeling a searing pain in his side. He fell back, his vision blurring as he looked at Christy. Her eyes went wide, tears streaming down her face.

Mark stood, panting, holding the gun. He looked at Dan, who was struggling to breathe, then turned to Christy. "You're coming with me," he growled, grabbing her wrist. "Guess this is game over for you, Pen Pal." and aimed the weapon at Dan's head. . . Mark pulled the Trigger, BOOM! . . .

Dan's vision darkened. Everything went black.

Chapter 21

A New Perspective

. . .

BOOM!

. . .

The crashing sound of thunder rolled over the Arizona house, waking Dan with a start. His eyes flung open, heart pounding in his chest. He blinked against the dim light, the storm's deep rumble reverberating through the room, shaking the windows as rain lashed against them as the grandfather clock struck the last note of the hour. Dan struggled to make sense of his surroundings; a dense fog clouded his mind, and a sharp, unrelenting pain in his head was like a relentless storm.

"No, no, no!" he murmured, his breaths shallow and erratic like a fish out of water. Pressing his palms against the cool, unforgiving floor, his feet found the chilling ground beneath him. Memories from before surged back like jagged shards of glass, slicing through his consciousness. "Christy!" Dan shouted, his voice echoing in the emptiness as he looked around frantically, the image of Mark and the terrifying gunshot flashing in his mind. He winced, a stabbing ache piercing through his temple with every movement.

"It can't be real. Please, God, don't let it be," he chanted under his breath, desperation lacing each word. His trembling hand reached to the back of his head, where he discovered a throbbing bump, smaller than he had initially recalled. His knees buckled as he attempted to stand, a sharp cry escaping him as he grasped the edge of the couch to steady himself.

His eyes darted around the room, scanning for any clues of the night's events—where was Mark? Where had the others gone? Was Christy safe? The grandfather clock stood silent, its hands pointing to seven o'clock in the morning. The house was eerily empty, a ghostly stillness hanging in the air.

"What... what is this?" Dan muttered, his voice quavering with uncertainty. Could it all have been just a dream? A terrifying, vivid nightmare? He shook his head, trying to untangle the web of confusion. He remembered the screams, the palpable fear, the searing pain—it had felt undeniably real. The storm outside seemed to retreat, the rumbling thunder fading into the distance. Dan shuffled toward the bar, leaning heavily on it for support. He glanced back at the spot where he had fallen, searching for any trace of blood. But there was nothing.

Slowly, the reality settled within him like a heavy fog lifting. He was home—back in his own custom house. As much as he wished to believe that everything that had transpired was merely a figment of his imagination, the emotions clung to him stubbornly, refusing to release their grip. Part of him felt an overwhelming sense of relief, while another part ached with a deep longing—for Christy, for the connection they had shared. He glanced at his watch, disbelief washing over him. Could it be true that nearly 48 hours had passed? Had he been out for that long? His slightly soiled undergarments provided a disconcerting confirmation.

Dan took a deep breath, forcing himself upstairs to his room. His digital clock was flashing because of the storm. He needed to clear his head. He made his way to the bathroom, taking some aspirin to ease the pain. A cool shower followed, the water grounding him to the present, him holding himself steady with one hand on the wall. The water was now warmer, washing away the dizziness and traces of old blood which swirled around his feet before disappearing down the drain. He shampooed softly over the slight bump on his head. His thoughts drifting back to the dream. As painful as it had been, it had also shown him something important—how much he loved Christy, and how much he wanted her in his life.

"What did Christy say?" Dan whispered to himself, chuckling as he remembered. "She already likes me, right? I got this." He smiled, feeling a surge of determination. He didn't need to rely on the duplicator anymore—he needed to trust in himself, in the feelings they had shared.

He headed down to his lab. The enormous eyes of a rabbit stared back at him from its cage, twitching its nose at him. Dan smiled, rubbing its forehead. "Good to see you, little guy," he said softly, filling up his empty dish bowl and replacing the water.

Dan turned his attention to the duplicator. The sight that greeted him was surreal. The duplicating machine sat, fully assembled, as if nothing had happened. Curiosity tugged at him, and he ran a few tests.

"What was it again? Ah, the static field interference," he recalled while putting the machine back together according to his memory, then switched on the power. Grabbing an apple, he savored its sweetness. He accessed the log of a previously scanned apple and entered it into the replication program. The machine hummed, and a faint, fuzzy image appeared above the plate. Dan's heart raced with anticipation, his eyes glued to the platform as continued to spin.

The image wavered, then collapsed into a puddle of mush. Dan sighed, shaking his head. "Not even applesauce," he repeated from before, as He cleaned up the mess, a wry smile tugging at his lips. "It was for the best," he thought. He powered down the machine and dismantled it.

Dan heading upstairs. He needed fresh air, something to take his mind off everything. He walked out to the mailbox, surprised at the stack of envelopes stuffed inside. As he flipped through them, the phone inside the house rang.

Dan hurried back in, just in time to hear Steven's voice on the answering machine. "Hey, Danny boy! You are screening your calls!" Steven chuckled. "I thought I'd finally take you up on your invite and come see you this weekend. I scheduled the entire weekend open in case you said yes."

A smile spread across Dan's face. He picked up the phone, his heart lifting at the familiar voice. "Hey, Steven. I'd love that. I could use some familiar company."

"Aww, did someone miss me?" Steven joked.

"Yeah," Dan responded honestly, the words catching in his throat. He hadn't realized just how much he had needed to hear from his friend.

"Whoa, okay, didn't expect that. What's up, man? You good?"

Dan hesitated, then smiled. "This coming weekend is perfect,"

"I've got a long story to share with you, one that's almost unbelievable."

Chapter 22

Love in the Afternoon

THE NEXT DAY, DAN was still feeling the echoes of the dream, his emotions raw. He was sitting on the couch in his robe when the doorbell rang. He groaned, not expecting anyone he thought could be salesman or religious folks coming to spread some good news about how the entire world has it all wrong, but they fortunately carry the truth. The ringing persisted. Sighing, he trudged to the door, then realizing it could be Steven. Not bothering turning on the LCD peeping monitor, Dan hurried, opening it—and froze.

"Hey," Christy beamed, her eyes sparkling.

Dan blinked, his heart skipping a beat. "Christy!," he choked, pulling her into a tight hug. "You're here," he whispered, his voice breaking. She laughed softly, hugging him back.

"Wow, okay! I missed you too," Christy said, her tone light. Dan pulled away, his eyes wide with disbelief and a big grin.

"It's so good to see you," he said, his grin widening. "Please, come in."

Christy stepped inside, looking around. "This place looks amazing, Dan. It feels so cozy," she said, her eyes sweeping across the room.

Dan smiled, closed the door, his heart swelling. "I'm glad you think so." He watched as her gaze landed on the bar, a curious smile playing on her lips.

"You drink?" she asked, nodding towards the whiskey bottle.

Dan chuckled. "No, not really. Tried it once—not my thing," he said, placing his hand on his head. Christy laughed, her cheeks turning pink.

Suddenly, a loud voice came from outside. "HEY! Open the door, dingbat. It's hot out here!" Dan and Christy both turned toward the door, startled.

"Tina!" Christy exclaimed, rushing to let her friend in. Tina entered, her face flushed, frowning playfully.

"What gives? You two get together, and you forget about the rest of us," Tina teased, nudging Dan as she walked by. Dan laughed, pulling Tina into a hug. She stiffened, then patted his back awkwardly. "Hey! What's gotten into you!?" she mumbled, hugging him back.

Dan let her go, his eyes shining. "I'm just happy to see you both," he said sincerely.

Tina eyed him suspiciously, but her expression softened. "Well, don't get all mushy on me," she said, rolling her eyes. "We just stopped by on the way to my eye appointment."

"How'd you find me?" Dan smiled curiously.

"Tina said you had built a house on our favorite spot up the mountains and I knew!, I just had to see for myself and it's so beautiful!" Christy smiled, looking back at Dan. "but mostly, I wanted to see you," she said softly.

Dan's heart swelled. "How about a late lunch or early dinner tomorrow or today?" he asked, his voice hopeful.

Christy's eyes lit up, and she nodded. "I'd love that!. I already told Tina I would go with her to her appointment but I could be available after, Pick me up at my parent's house a little after one. "

"Perfect," Dan said, smiling. He opened the door for them, watching as they made their way to the car. Tina paused, turning to Christy with a knowing smirk.

"He seems different," they giggled when they both said it at the same time. Tina's voice is almost teasing. Christy blushed, glancing back at Dan, still standing by the door, there smiling.

"He didn't even stutter once." Dan heard Christy say before getting into the car.

Dan closed the door, leaning against it. He felt a warmth spreading through him—hope, love, excitement. He remembered the dream version of Christy.

***

Dan wanted the day to be unforgettable, something that would make Christy smile long after it was over. He had thought of every detail, mapping out each moment in his head, determined to make this perfect. Dan had researched for what felt like hours, combing through maps, reviews, and hidden spots just outside the city—somewhere quiet, scenic, untouched by the usual noise of everyday life. When he finally found it, something clicked. He remembered Christy's old letters—how she once described a place she saw in a magazine or a documentary, with trees that dipped over a stream and wildflowers that didn't look real. It was so clear. Almost eerily so. The spot matched her words like a memory came to life.

Hurrying upstairs, he got dressed, making sure he looked his best. As he grabbed his keys, he took a deep breath. 'Don't be nervous. Just be you.' He could almost hear Christy's voice saying, a reassuring echo from his dream.

Dan drove to the store and picked up a classic woven picnic basket and a red and white checkered blanket—because what was a picnic without the proper setup? He made his way to the deli and ordered an assortment of small sandwiches, specifically asking for the crusts to be cut off. It felt like a ridiculous detail, but something about it made him grin.

He then stopped by a tiny bakery and picked up two delicate fruit tarts, wrapped neatly in a box. If this was going to be a memory worth keeping, it had to be more than just sandwiches.

Back at his car, he carefully arranged the picnic basket, tucking a small bag of ice under the sparkling grape juice to keep it chilled. He draped his jacket over it, making sure it stayed a surprise. The two plastic champagne flutes clinked softly as he adjusted them.

With a last glance at his checklist, he set off for Christy's house.

When he arrived, Christy greeted him at the door, her characteristic warmth immediately settling on his nerves.

"Hey, you made it!" she beamed.

"You look wonderful," Dan said, his voice filled with admiration. Christy blushed, her smile widening.

"So, what's the plan? There's this pizza place I've been wanting to try," she said excitedly.

Dan chuckled, shaking his head. "Not today. I've got something else in mind."

Her eyes sparkled with curiosity, but she didn't press further. She simply slid into the passenger seat, her excitement radiating through the car.

Twenty minutes later, their conversation rested as they pulled off onto a secluded road. Christy's eyes widened.

"Dan... where are we going?" she asked, watching the bushes and heavy rocks give way to a breathtaking clearing. A tiny waterfall cascaded down into a serene stream, a faint rainbow arching over it in the mist.

Dan smiled, pulling the car to a stop. "You'll see." The scenery was much different from he remembered in his dream, yet it held its own breathtaking beauty.

Christy stepped out and immediately twirled on her feet, lifting her arms toward the sky. "This place is Magical!"

Dan grabbed the basket and led her under the shade of a tree. As he spread out the picnic blanket, she sat down eagerly, watching with curiosity.

He placed the basket in front of her. She smiled seeing the assortments of small sandwiches inside. She reached into the basket, pulling out a sandwich. Christy grinned as she unwrapped it. "Not knowing what kind it is... that's part of the fun, right?" She took a bite, her expression one of exaggerated suspense before lighting up. "Mmm, turkey and cranberry! Nice pick."

Dan smirked. "Beginner's luck."

Then, with a bit of dramatic flair, he pulled out the bottle of sparkling grape juice, revealing it from beneath his jacket.

Christy's brow lifted. "Oh? Are we celebrating something?"

"You tell me," Dan said, popping the cork with a satisfying 'pop!'

She gasped playfully as he poured the fizzy liquid into the cups. But when she brought it to her lips, recognition flickered in her eyes.

"You... remembered... How did you remember? I think I might have mentioned it just once in a letter, and I can't even recall it clearly, but you remembered," she whispered, looking at him with admiration.

Dan sensed a shift inside himself upon seeing her expression, and a smile that conveyed, 'I did, your someone worth remembering for.'

For a moment, the world slowed. Christy set down her glass and looked at him with something deeper than gratitude—something unspoken yet undeniable. "You seem so different, in a good way, more confident." She smiled boldly.

"You are so amazing, so beautiful," Dan found himself saying before he even realized the words had escaped.

She blinked in surprise, her cheeks tinged pink. Before either of them could think too much about it, Dan leaned in, wrapping an arm around her waist.

The breeze rustled through the bushes; the stream hummed its quiet song, and time held still as they melted into the moment.

The rest of the afternoon unfolded in a way that felt almost unreal—like a dream they had stepped into together.

They explored the stream, skipping stones and daring each other to cross it without getting their shoes wet.

"Bet you can't beat me to the top! Whoever touches the highest point first wins!" Christy taunted, her eyes flashing with excitement.

Dan smirked. "Oh, it's on."

Before he could blink, she darted off, her feet kicking up leaves and dirt as she sprinted toward the rocky incline. Dan bolted after her, pushing harder with every stride. She was fast—really fast—but he was determined.

Halfway up, he surged ahead, passing her with a triumphant grin. "See you at the top!"

"Oh, no you don't!" she shot back, quickening her pace.

As the incline steepened, Christy's steps faltered slightly. Without thinking, Dan reached back, grabbed her wrist, stabilizing her from fall. She looked at him with surprise and gratitude. She smiled, grabbing his wrist then slowly pulling back until her hands were in his. They walked with her fingers slipping into his, climbing up together.

For a moment, they weren't racing anymore. Their hands held firm, their movements in sync, and Dan couldn't ignore the way it felt—natural, effortless, right?

But then, just as they neared the peak, Christy suddenly lets go, sprinting ahead with a mischievous laugh. She reached out, tapping the highest rock first.

"I win!" she declared breathlessly, turning to him with a victorious grin.

Dan exhaled, shaking his head with a chuckle. "You would pull something like that."

She nudged him playfully. "A win's a win, Dan."

Dan approached her with a bold stride, his towering presence giving him the upper hand as he reached up and slammed his hand against the rock just above hers. "I win!" he declared, his eyes burning with an intense gaze that pierced into hers, adding with a teasing yet commanding tone, "A win's a win." Christy, momentarily stunned, felt a shock of realization as she realized he had indeed beaten her to the highest point. In one swift, decisive motion, he wrapped his arm around her waist, yanking her close with an undeniable urgency. "And now for my prize," he murmured, his voice low and charged, as he leaned in to claim a kiss with a searing intensity. Her eyes fluttered open slightly, but she surrendered completely to the moment, dissolving into it.

Later, as the sky blazed into a tapestry of fiery blues and oranges, they lay intertwined on the picnic blanket, watching the sunset's fierce beauty. Christy nestled closer, resting her head on his shoulder, seeking the warmth of his presence. Their hands found each other with an electric magnetism, fingers weaving together as if they had always been meant to fit.

"I never want this to end," she murmured, her voice a whisper against the vibrant backdrop.

Dan pressed a lingering kiss to the top of her head, his lips a promise. "Then let's make every second count."

Christy's breath caught, and then—just like that—his lips met hers in a soft, lingering kiss.

Just as everything seemed serene and peaceful, a single buzzing sound interrupted the quiet.

Dan flinched, swatting at his ear. "Ugh—what was that?"

Christy sat up, watching him with amusement. "Bug got you?"

He smacked at his cheek again, groaning. "I think it's targeting me on purpose."

Christy burst into a fit of laughter, nearly doubling over. "Well, don't hurt it! Nature has chosen you!" Dan gave her an exasperated look before dramatically wrapping the picnic blanket around himself like a protective shield. "Okay, okay," she wheezed between laughs. "We should probably start packing up before they recruit reinforcements." Still chuckling, they gathered everything, their laughter carrying into the night.

On the drive home, Christy filled the car with warmth, reminiscing about the day, reliving the best parts. Dan listened, nodding and smiling, feeling something deep settle inside him.

As they pulled into her driveway, she turned to him with a soft smile. "This was perfect. Thank you."

Dan reached out, tucking a loose strand of hair behind her ear. "Anytime, Soon I hope."

She lingered for just a moment before opening the door. "Goodnight, Dan."

"Goodnight, Christy," he whispered as she disappeared inside.

As he drove off, the distant smell of rain filled the air, and for once, he wasn't thinking about what tomorrow held.

Because today?

Today was perfect.

***

The following morning, Dan woke up to the soft hum of sunlight filtering through his blinds. Stretching lazily, he dragged himself out of bed and shuffled toward the kitchen. As he poured himself a cup of juice, the blinking red light on his answering machine caught his attention.

With a raised brow, he pressed play.

Tina's voice burst through the speaker, filled with energy and unmistakable amusement. "Well, well—looks like you worked some kind of magic! Not sure what you did, but she's broken up with Mark. Good job, kiddo!"

Dan froze, captivated by the moment.

A slow, stunned smile spread across his face. A wave of hope filled his chest.

Tina's voice continued, practically buzzing with excitement as if charged with electric energy. "Seriously, Dan, whatever you said or did—it really made an impact. She came over last night, and I haven't seen her this confident about anything in ages. You might actually be onto something here. Don't screw it up, dingbat!" Dan let out a breathless laugh, shaking his head in amusement. Classic Tina, always knowing how to tease him just right.

His mind drifted back to the day before, replaying the scene in vivid detail—the way Christy had looked at him with eyes full of warmth and curiosity, the way they had laughed together, each moment stretching out as if time itself had softened and slowed down just for them. They had created a memory together, one that was rich with meaning and vibrancy, a memory that, somehow, had changed everything.

Dan eagerly awaited Steven's visit as the weekend approached. He knew Steven would have plenty to say, but Dan was eager to share every detail of his experience, to express just how much it had transformed him, and to admit how right Steven had been all along.

For the first time in a long while, the future didn't feel like an uncertain haze. It felt alive with possibility, like a horizon painted with the colors of hope and promise.

Chapter 23

Playful Banter and New Beginnings

THE WEEKEND FINALLY ARRIVED, and with it, the familiar rumble of Steven's car outside. Dan smiled to himself and headed to the door, opening it just as Steven approached, two bags of BBQ supplies in hand and his usual mischievous grin plastered across his face.

"Hey, Steven!" Dan greeted, pulling him into a quick hug.

"Wouldn't miss this for the world," Steven said, giving him a playful slap on the back. "Figured we should break in the new place properly—got some ribs, some burgers, even a variety of vegetables to grill that you love."

"You know me too well." Dan chuckled and motioned for him to come in. As they set the bags down in the kitchen,

Steven leaned back against the counter, giving Dan a curious look. "So, whatever happened to that duplicator project, you were convinced you were on the brink before moving out here?"

Dan's smile faded slightly, replaced with something quieter—almost reflective. "Funny you ask," he said. "You wouldn't believe it," Dan laughed a little. "The other night I hit my head, and when I came to, I had this dream—this insanely vivid, surreal dream—and in it. . . I figured out how to finish the duplicator."

Steven's eyes widened. "Wait—are you serious? You finished it?"

Dan nodded. "In the dream, I got it working. Actually working."

Steven raised his eyebrows, curiosity fully piqued. "So. . . where is it? I mean, did you build it in real life after that? Can I see it?"

Dan hesitated, then gave a slow nod toward the China Cabinet. "What's left of it, yeah? I dismantled part of it."

They stepped into the elevator, "Ahh, the China cabinet, you like it, that was my idea" Steven mentioned as they went down to the Lab, where a few scattered components remained on a bench, wires bundled, and parts sorted into bins. Steven eyed the pile, frowning thoughtfully.

Dan gave Steven a quick recap of everything that had happened—the new place, Christy, and that strange dream he couldn't shake.

"So... this thing actually produced weird apple sludge or something?!" Steven asked, poking at one piece with a screwdriver.

Dan gave a short laugh. "Something like that. It got. . . close."

Dan continued, "But in the dream, I got it to work. I used it. . . to duplicate Christy." Steven blinked in suspense while Dan continued. "She was flawless," a mix of awe and sadness in his tone. "And I fell for her. Hard."

Steven took that in, quiet for a moment. "Man... that's intense. So... what else happened?"

Dan exhaled. "I married the double. We ran away together. I was happy—at least, I thought I was. But the original. . . her life unraveled. Mark got involved. And in the end, he shot me. I woke up drenched in sweat, shaken. It all felt so real."

Steven gave a low whistle. "So, it was like an epiphany."

"Exactly," Dan said. "And when I woke up, I knew—this thing couldn't exist. Even if I could build it. . . this world would just find all the wrong ways to use it."

Steven nodded slowly. "Heavy stuff, man." Then, with a grin, "Still. . . you did almost pull it off. If anyone could've done it, it's you."

Dan smirked. "Well, I dismantled it. Piece by piece. It's gone."

"Man, I get it. A machine like that—" He placed a hand on Dan's shoulder, his voice steady. "You did the right thing, Dan. . . But hey," Steven added with a crooked smile, "we should've just built it for ourselves and used it for all the wrong reasons."

Dan burst into laughter. "Oh yeah, for sure. Chaos in a bottle." As they made their way back up the elevator.

Steven looked over more intently. "So, that dream really got to you, didn't it?"

Dan responded with a genuine, serene smile. "Yeah, it did. It's odd," he said softly, wonder clear in his voice. "How our subconscious clings to bits of the past—silently, like shadows—only to bring them back, as vivid as ever, when we least expect it."

The China Cabinet closed quietly behind them. They shared a few more laughs, clinking their glasses together. The duplicator—and that strange dream—were finally history.

Steven took a sip, watching Dan over the rim of his cup. "And what about Christy? The real one, the date, that message on the answering machine—it all sounded like a win."

Dan's expression softened, his smile sincere. "It was. And she's... wonderful."

Grinning, Steven nudged him with his elbow. "I'd like to meet the girl who made it all worthwhile for you. Maybe I'll get to meet her? Have you told her about the dream?"

"Not yet. I'm not sure if I will, maybe someday when everything's settled," Dan replied, as they relaxed in the kitchen filled with the aroma of sizzling barbecue, laughter, and the scent of spices and smoke. Just as they settled in, there was a knock at the door, and Dan turned to Steven with a surprised grin. "Looks like you're not the only one who dropped by," he said, opening the door to reveal Christy and Tina, both beaming.

"Surprise!" Christy exclaimed, her eyes sparkling. "I hope it's okay. We stopped by. I brought you a carrot cake I made."

"Of course it's okay, just give me a little warning when Tina stops by." Dan tried to joke

"Good one, genius!" Tina responded, making Dan blush. Christy giggled. "Smells great in here. What you got cooking." Tina said while taking in the scent.

"My friend Steven is here visiting, cooking up a storm in the kitchen." Dan said, closing the door

"Well, well, looks like you've got more company than you thought, Dan," Steven said, grinning. He stepped forward, catching sight of the two women. Christy smiled warmly, but Tina's eyes zeroed in on Steven with mild curiosity.

"Oh, you must be Steven, the one Dan said kept him sane at work," Christy said, giving him a friendly smile.

"That's me!" Steven replied, his attention flickering to Tina, who crossed her arms, eyebrows raised in mild amusement. "And you must be Tina, the infamous best friend who keeps everyone in line," Steven added, with a teasing glint in his eye.

"Infamous? Only if you ask the wrong people," Tina shot back, a sly smile tugging at her lips. "Dan said you were some kind of genius inventor. But then again, he exaggerates."

"Exaggerate?! From this modest guy?" Steven patted Dan's back, pretending to take offense, placing a hand over his heart. "Please, it's true my inventions are pretty impressive—if I do say so myself." He gave her a mock serious look, leaning closer. "And I bet you've never met anyone as impressive as me."

"Oh, I've met plenty," Tina replied, tilting her head. "They just haven't lasted long enough to make a second impression."

Dan and Christy exchanged an amused glance, sensing the playful spark between their friends.

"Oh, now that sounds like a challenge," Steven replied, his voice tinged with curiosity. "I've got staying power, though."

"We'll see," Tina shot back with a mischievous glint. She gave him a once-over, barely concealing a smirk. "I hear you've got quite the reputation. You must be as clever as Dan says."

"Only on my good days," Steven replied with a chuckle. "What about you? Dan mentioned you have a...gift for reading people."

Tina shrugged, maintaining her mysterious aura. "I don't like to brag. But I'd say I'm pretty good at reading intentions. Yours are... interesting," she added, her gaze sharp.

"Oh, now you've got me curious," Steven said, flashing a grin. "Let's just say I have a hard time hiding my intentions. And right now, I intend to find out exactly how much you think you know."

Dan and Christy could barely hold back their amusement as they watched the exchange.

Steven seemed genuinely intrigued, his usual confidence tempered by a hint of admiration. He and Tina bantered back and forth, their exchanges growing more playful with each quip, until finally, the four of them headed out onto the back patio to enjoy the afternoon.

As they sat together, the conversation turned to travel. Tina mentioned her love of wandering off the beaten path, exploring places with rich history and hidden charm.

"Really?" Steven asked, his voice laced with genuine interest. "That's what I love to do. I once spent two weeks in a tiny mountain town, totally unplanned. I just let the place take me where it wanted. The freedom. . . there's nothing like it."

Tina's eyes widened, her expression softening. "I did something like that last summer. A tiny town in the middle of nowhere, where no one knew me. It felt like I was living a whole new life for a while."

Their eyes met, a silent understanding passing between them. Dan and Christy watched, sensing the connection deepened. There was something unspoken, a feeling of recognition. Tina looked down, a slight blush coloring her cheeks, and Steven's confident expression softened as well.

"So... think you'd ever go on another unplanned adventure?" Steven asked, his voice a touch quieter.

"Maybe," Tina replied, a slight smile playing on her lips. "Depends on the company." She looked back up, meeting his gaze.

"Then I guess I'll have to make sure you're stuck with the best," he replied, leaning back with a grin.

Steven gave Tina a small nudge, directing her attention back to Dan and Christy. They exchanged knowing smiles, recognizing the moment for what it was. Dan and Christy sat close, enveloped in a comfortable silence, a peace that spoke volumes more than words. Everything was falling into place, fitting together perfectly like pieces of a long-awaited puzzle. The past—the duplicator, the dream, the uncertainty—all seemed to fade away, leaving only this new beginning.

Dan's eyes met hers, and in that glance, they both knew that nothing else mattered except where they were right now with each other.

Dan smiled at Christy, a look that held no hesitation or fear, just a pure, unspoken promise. She returned it, her eyes warm and bright, reflecting the joy of finding something real and lasting. It was as if time itself slowed, allowing them to savor this feeling of completeness, a harmony that transcended any need for conversation. The air around them felt light, electric with possibility. They didn't need to say anything. Their expressions conveyed everything—a shared understanding, a silent assurance, a commitment to this chapter of their lives. They paused in perfect synchronicity, contentment washing over them like a soft, soothing wave.

Even Steven and Tina, watching them, felt the resonance of it. It was like witnessing the quiet power of a promise fulfilled, the culmination of a journey that had been long and uncertain. Dan and Christy were truly in their moment—alive in the present, sure of what they had. It was authentic and unclouded, a clarity that comes once.

This was their story now—their future, their love, their life to build and cherish. Together, they were ready to embrace whatever came next!

The future, it seemed, was just beginning.

The End

David Nevarez

A Note from the Author

Thank you for reading *Dreamer: Cloning Love*.

This story has been a deeply personal journey for me, and I'm honored that you chose to spend your time with these characters and their struggles. If something in this story resonated with you—if it made you reflect, smile, or feel seen—I consider that the highest reward.

If you enjoyed this book, please consider leaving a review or sharing it with a friend. Every kind word, rating, and recommendation makes a difference and helps keep stories like this alive.

With gratitude,

David Nevarez

About the Author

David Nevarez is the co-founder of D&F Books and a writer of emotionally immersive science fiction. His debut novel, *Dreamer: Cloning Love*, explores love, longing, and the quiet courage it takes to act on what matters most.

David lives and writes in California, where he continues creating stories that honor imagination, emotional truth, and human connection.